WHAT HAPPENED TO US?

NORTH AMERICA'S
FALL FROM GREATNESS

Richard H Shaw

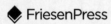

FriesenPress

Suite 300 - 990 Fort St
Victoria, BC, V8V 3K2
Canada

www.friesenpress.com

This broad, economically and politically inspired narrative looks at North America's place in the world since early in the twentieth century, focusing on the issues of energy security, political leadership in Washington and Ottawa, and Middle East turbulence. This is a work of historically-centred fiction. The author's imagination is used to place fictional characters into actual historical events in a fictitious manner in five short stories. Any reference to actual persons, living or dead, as well as the historical events, is presented for the sake of narrative, and in good faith. No defamation or libel is intended.

ISBN
978-1-5255-2248-2 (Hardcover)
978-1-5255-2249-9 (Paperback)
978-1-5255-2250-5 (eBook)

1. FICTION, POLITICAL

Distributed to the trade by The Ingram Book Company

ADDENDUM TO THE NOVEL: *WHAT HAPPENED TO US?*
REGARDING NEGATIVE REACTIONS TO THIS NOVEL
(From the author: May 31, 2018)

The novel has been in the public for just over a week, and it's already clear I should clarify the intent behind the book. It was written because of my love for Canada, the United States, and North America, and my concern for the long-term future of our descendants. In my opinion, significant changes are required in the governance of our nations and I've chosen to look at history through fictional characters in an effort to explain that opinion.

An accusation of anti-Semitism has been directed at the novel by a firm in New York. I consider that accusation a negative abstraction, designed to destroy one's credibility without explanation or support. In no way should the novel be seen as anti-Semitic. There are many scenes, involving Harry Grumner, Lord Conrad, Simon Ha-am, Simon's mother, and Adam Goldsilva, which are honestly and purposely pro-Jewish and consistent with historical realities. There are also scenes in the novel that reflect on Zionist influences over the past century; Zionism publically surfaced late in the 19th century, championed the 1917 Balfour Declaration, and played a critically positive role in battling Nazism from the mid-1930s until the end of WWII. I admit some confusion as to the full extent of Zionism's influences over western societies and the Jewish people today; if my confusion created fictional scenes that cause concern for the Jewish people and community, I apologize.

Following is what I hope readers take from the novel. First: the leaders of the United States and Canada have lost proper direction in their guardianship responsibilities. Second: today powerful and unaccountable lobbyists, sponsored by 'very-big-money' from who knows where, have far too much influence over officials elected to govern our societies. Third: since the end of the Cold War in the early 1990s, U.S. support of or none-action against the distribution of modern weapons throughout the world has placed the whole world on the brink of war(s). Fourth: since the 1980s, the U.S. has spent far too much 'veto' influence at the UN in support of modern-Israel while that nation continues to avoid meaningful peace efforts in Palestine. In my opinion, our descendants will be much better off if those things are somehow reversed. If some readers choose to target that thought with the anti-Semitic abstraction, so be it; I only feel sorry for them and wish their descendants peace and happiness in the future.

TABLE OF CONTENTS

INTRODUCTION BY AUTHOR

Thank you for opening this book. Before you start reading, let me explain why I wrote the story.

I'm an eighty year old Canadian, deeply thankful for the peace, safety, freedom, and opportunities of living in North America. A lot has happened during those eighty years: World War Two was fought and won, the United States and Canada led the world economies to recovery and great wealth, and by the early-1980s North America appeared to be in the final stages of an effort to become self-sufficient in energy and lead the world to peace.

That effort became snagged, and by the mid-1990s I was wondering why. I'm sure one of the primary causes of the snag was a major shift in our North American political and business ethos. For example, our 'business model' following WWII was one of strong customer service and employee loyalty, clear delegation of meaningful responsibility and accountable authority, conservative monetary policies, efforts to improve employee productivity, and focus on supporting national needs; but by the early-1990s that 'business model' had clearly changed to one of strong centralized authorities often involving international strategies and controls, a focus on short-term earnings and growth rates, replacement of loyal staff with consultants and hi-tech machines, highly levered investments without clear financial accountability, obscene executive bonuses, leaders shifting personal assets out-of-country to avoid taxes, too-big-to-fail corporations, etc. Right now, the governments of Canada and the U.S. are tearing apart longstanding relationships; and at risk of involvement in new military conflicts in Asia and the Middle East. This novel may provide important perspectives on what got us in this situation.

The novel comprises five short stories, each moving quickly through many years of history, keeping details to a minimum while touching on events in a way that might encourage readers to dig deeper. The characters deal with some tough stuff, many contentious issues. At times, because those characters are living in different parts of the world and during different times, their behaviour and expressions may seem 'politically incorrect' in the context of forgotten history or our customs today. At no time during the writing of the novel was defamation or libel intended, and I assure all readers that the character dialogue and background narrative is presented in good faith. My primary focus and objective is to inform, to persuade both Canadians and Americans to think longer-term than the unrelenting media clutter of today; and to provide encouragement to thoughtful readers who are themselves interested in history and desire a North American future that is aimed toward a great and moral prosperity that will be safe, peaceful, inclusive, and personally motivating for our descendants.

I hope you enjoy the book.

The Author
May, 2018

STORY 1

THE UNITED STATES OF AMERICA

CHAPTER 1

MONTANA TO WASHINGTON

Late 1982; San Francisco, California

"Well, dear!" Her voice was bright and happy. "What have you got in store for our family now?" Donna turned with a smile and looked proudly at Troy as he brought their Ford Torino to a stop in the front driveway of their new home in the upscale suburban community south of San Francisco.

The family was a handsome foursome. Troy and Donna Rogers, both thirty-eight years old, had been married for seventeen years. Their close friends often compared their looks to famous Hollywood favourites Clark Gable and Jean Simmons. Their daughter, fifteen-year-old Leslie, scrambled out her side of the back seat with their scottie-poo dog, Curly, and both joyfully raced toward the wide expanse of lawn. Jeff, two years younger, leaned forward from the back seat and held his open right hand toward his dad. "How about the key to the front door, Dad?" He took it and ran to the house.

Donna's question seemed quite appropriate for this family, whose lives, to date, had been one adventure after the other. She and Troy had been good friends during their public and high school days in Great Falls, Montana. Donna was teaching in the city's public school system for a year before they married, soon after Troy's graduation as a mechanical engineer from Butte University. The day after their marriage, they were off to the west coast for Troy to begin his career with EPC Contractor, one of the largest engineering and construction companies in the United States. It had not been an easy beginning. Troy became discouraged and anxious about the confines of a pure engineering focus and was seriously considering leaving his job when Donna announced her pregnancy. Instead of quitting, he worked harder and focused on broadening his capabilities and scope of interests through evening and correspondence classes at Stanford University's business MBA program. Executives at EPC Contractor recognized Troy's determination, and his responsibilities were progressively broadened. In 1970, the family was transferred to Houston, Texas. In 1976, the company assigned Troy to Edmonton, Alberta, with responsibility for securing and executing project construction contracts throughout western and northern Canada. It was part of the extensive efforts by major Canadian and U.S. corporations to deal with a serious North American energy crisis created by the Arab oil weapon following the 1973 Yom Kippur War. It was an extremely challenging work environment for Troy, and the family loved living in Edmonton. However, by 1982, the pressures created by the Arab oil weapon began to disappear, the world-wide energy crisis ended, and the need for Canadian mega-project energy developments ceased. And now, Troy was transferring back to EPC Contractor's head office with executive responsibilities for managing the company's liaison with local, state, and federal government offices and agencies throughout the United States.

The new community was active and caring, and both Troy and Donna soon became strong and popular participants in church, school, and other community affairs. The academic talents, athletic capabilities, and fine personalities the teenagers had developed in Edmonton opened opportunities for new friendships, and they quickly fit in to the new environment.

In mid-summer 1985, three years after the move back to the United States from Canada, Troy and Donna attended a fundraising gala for Vice-President George H. W. Bush. Troy, now forty-one and somewhat greyed at the temples, had the appearance and presence of a leader. Donna, the same age, was strikingly beautiful, with her dark eyes framed by long black eyelashes and black wavy hair that covered the back of her neck and was expertly shaped to show the small diamond earrings she often wore. The couple caught the attention of many influential people. Later in the evening, Troy unexpectedly found himself in a small group of California Republicans who were talking about the growing influence of "neocons" in Washington. Troy had heard the term used only a few times. *They're a powerful and influential group within Reagan's administration*, he told himself. Most in the gathering were quite concerned about that growing influence. As discussion shifted to what might happen after the Reagan Administration left the White House in early 1989, two senior Republicans took Troy aside and quizzed him on whether or not he'd be interested in running for the party's candidacy in the Federal House of Representatives in 1988.

During the following months, Troy and Donna considered the idea of Washington politics and the impact such a move would have on their lives and long-term security. They eventually decided Troy should pursue any meaningful opportunity to serve the nation and he advised the Republican leaders of his interest. It took another year before leading party members told him they were interested.

After that, he approached the president of EPC Contractor about the idea and was assured the company would honour his decision, and wanted him to continue handling his current responsibilities until he was elected to and settled in Congress. The next big step was early in April 1987, when Troy was the headliner at a small gathering of key Republican leaders at the Fairmont Hotel in San Francisco.

Two small conference rooms were reserved in a section of the third floor of the hotel. The elevator dedicated to service that section was manned by security guards. Guards were also located at the single stairwell. One of the rooms was arranged with four circular dining tables, each set for six. The other room had a large bar attended by security personnel; everyone gathered there for cocktails before dinner. After the cocktail hour, they moved from the bar to the dining area and the door between the two rooms was closed.

The host guided Troy to the head table and addressed the gathering. "Ladies and gentlemen, I'm pleased to offer you this opportunity to check out one of our leading candidates for the seat that will be vacated by Representative Pickel in early 1989. You have all met Troy Rogers and are aware of his impressive business background. It's important that we take this opportunity to thoroughly understand what policy thinking is behind his powerful and handsome exterior. That is the purpose of this gathering. I want frank questions, answers, and dialogue." He gestured with his left hand. "Let's have one question per table, and go around the horn again until we've covered everyone." He pointed to the far table on his left. "Mr. Stark, would you please get us started."

Stark stood and nodded toward the Chairman. "Thank you, Mr. Chairman." He was a big man with a tough but pleasant demeanour. "Mr. Rogers, I want to start by thanking you for your interest in becoming our House representative in Washington. I'd like to know, do you have any idea of the lobby pressures you will be facing in Washington, and if you do, how would you hope to deal with them?"

Troy was not sure whether he should sit or stand when addressing the questions. He stood, quite nervous. "I've heard a lot of rumours about the lobbyists in the corridors of Congress." He managed a chuckle. "I expect there are rules regarding the practice and, of course, if I'm elected, I will honour those rules and traditions. Frankly, I expect that during my initial years in Congress, I'll be totally focused on the interests of my own constituents here in California." He paused. "I guess there's an important fundamental guideline that will always govern what I do; I will never support anything that is not clearly intended to benefit our nation."

Stark nodded his thanks as a lady at the next table leaned forward. "Good luck with that, Mr. Rogers! Most of those lobbyists don't care what's good for America." There were a few grunts and snickers. "What do you think our country's top priorities should be?" she asked.

Troy's lips tightened involuntarily, the thumb of his right hand pressed lightly against his front teeth and a thoughtful squint came into his eyes. "Our domestic issues will always have top priority with me. International issues will be secondary, at least initially. I expect you want to hear some of both?"

It was a question and she nodded.

"I'd say there are three critically important domestic priorities right now, and they're all interrelated in one way or another. First is the need for America to once again become self-sufficient in energy.

Energy is fundamental to our national security and the strength of our economy. I consider it unacceptable for our nation to be as dependent on others for our oil supply as we are today.

"Second is the disturbing trend in the types of employment opportunities in America. I consider it a fundament responsibility for our leaders to create a proper economic and business environment, with related job opportunities, here in this country. At present, and for some time now, I feel things are going in the wrong direction. That might be due to the ambitious drive of corporations to cut costs and focus on short-term growth rates, as well as the fact that many of our manufacturing companies have shifted operations overseas in the interest of reducing expenses and avoiding American taxes. Those things all need our attention." He coughed to relieve a sudden tickle in his throat.

"Another domestic concern on my mind is the declining economies of so many of our great cities. In my opinion, that trend needs to be reversed." He reached for his glass of water.

A few softly applauded, and the next questioner stood. "There's considerable food for thought in what you say, Mr. Rogers. What about your thoughts on the international scene?"

Troy's eyes seemed to search the ceiling for an answer. "I want to repeat, domestic priorities are currently much more important to me than are international matters, provided we're not at war of course. The Soviet Union is weak and we seem to have won the Cold War." He paused for a few seconds. "And, as far as other key international issues are concerned, I'm repeating myself by pointing out that we depend upon other countries for over half of our crude oil needs, and we're constantly at odds with many of those countries! That's not good management."

Troy turned to the next table to indicate he was ready for another question.

"Mr. Rogers, what do you think of the challenges facing Israel?" the delegate asked.

Troy cleared his throat. "I think Israel is very well positioned and quite mature in its own management and development. Other than the need for Washington to strongly encourage a peaceful settlement in Palestine, I anticipate there is little we need to do."

The questioner huffed, obviously disturbed by Troy's answer as a hand was raised at the next table. "Mr. Rogers, what are your thoughts about the Pollard Affair?"

Troy took a deep breath. "I'm not sure I have all the facts on that case. I understand Jonathan Pollard and his wife have been working with our naval intelligence and spying for Israel over a two- or three-year period, and passing highly classified information regarding our nuclear weapons technology and programs to Mossad through the Israeli Embassy. I expect that is very serious—just don't know enough to comment further."

The questions continued for more than an hour and Troy handled many by referencing his fundamental priorities. There was a brief break and dinner was served. When it was over, most everyone thanked Troy for his thoughts and frankness. At the end of the evening, the chairman took him aside.

"That was a good evening, Troy. You gave us a lot to think about. Clearly a few of your points bothered some. We'll need to handle those concerns before finally deciding whether or not to select you to represent us in November '88. I'll get back to you ASAP."

In November 1987, the California Republican Party selected Troy Rogers to represent them down-ticket in the 1988 election for the House of Representatives in Washington.

January 1989; Washington, DC

Troy and Donna reacted to the wintry bite in the air as they walked out of the Dulles International Airport in Washington, DC. They were both forty-four years old and about to start a new and challenging chapter in their lives. They had decided to move from San Francisco to San Diego because Leslie was twenty-one and taking pre-med at the University of Southern California, and Jeff had just accepted his first job as a technician at the Scripps research facility in La Jolla. Their new home in San Diego's Old Town area was reasonably close to the San Diego airport. Donna and the children would live in San Diego, and she would fly to Washington whenever Troy needed her to be there.

Troy took Donna's hand and looked back to make sure the bellhop was following them with the luggage. A cold gust of wind whipped across their path. He turned up the collar of his coat with his free hand. Donna tucked in her chin and protected her bare neck with her free hand. Light flakes of snow blew haphazardly at their feet as they walked quickly to the government car waiting at the curb. Troy planned to tour the congressional buildings and become familiar with the routines of his office in the House during the next five days. While he was doing that Donna, who had never been to Washington, would look at apartment options.

Being anxious is just part of the routine, Troy thought. *If I weren't nervous, I'd be naive.* He undid the buttons of his coat, settled back into the plush seat, and turned to say something to Donna. She was looking out the window. He said nothing. *I hope she likes this place.* He reached over and took her hand.

The closer they got to Capitol Hill the more familiar the sites of Washington became. As they neared the Washington Monument, Donna pointed. "Is that the White House over there?"

"That's it," Troy said. "George Bush will be taking up residence in a few days."

Donna turned to look at Troy. "What do you think he'll do?" They had discussed the subject many times but expectations were continually changing.

Troy smiled, leaned over, and kissed her on the cheek. "That's the twenty-four-thousand-dollar question."

It did not take President George H. W. Bush long to establish his White House administration. At key positions were James Baker, Secretary of State; Dick Cheney, Secretary of Defence; and Colin Powell, Chairman of the Joint Chiefs of Staff at the Pentagon.

"I'm damn proud to be a small part of the team in Washington," Troy told Donna when he got back to San Diego for the summer break. And he repeatedly told local constituents, "There are lots of challenges we've got in Washington, but our nation can rest easy with the leadership we have in the White House."

In an effort to become involved in their new community, Donna had joined the family at the local United Church and, within a couple of weeks of arriving back for the summer, Troy joined the San Diego Golf Club. And very few of Troy's so-called vacation days went by without some form of social involvement with local political constituents.

During one of Troy's games at the Club a week before his return to Washington, his cart partner asked, "Troy, what do you think is the most important issue facing President Bush these days?"

"No question," Troy answered without hesitation. "A peace settlement needs to be finalized in Palestine. The Cold War is over, and the only thing holding back the march toward world-wide peace is the lack of that Middle East peace agreement."

On September 23, 1989, the White House and the Kremlin issued a joint statement expressing concern over the absence of a Middle East peace settlement, and on December 4, the United States supported a United Nations General Assembly resolution that called for the convening of an international peace conference on the Middle East, and reaffirmed President Bush's conviction that the question of Palestine was at the core of conflicts throughout the whole Middle East. However, when the White House announced in March 1990 that it planned to link a $400-million loan guarantee to Israel with the freezing of Jewish settlement construction in the Occupied Territories, Israel's Prime Minister Yitzhak Shamir and his supporters in the United States went on the warpath.

The old hands in Congress are telling me this is the beginning of a serious showdown between the Zionists and President Bush, Troy wrote in his diary at the end of March. He knew he did not fully appreciate the implications of what was happening and wished he was better versed on the full history of Israeli–American relations because, as he also wrote, *Middle East peace is critical to securing a stable and dependable oil supply for America's economy.* His follow-up discussions with others on Capitol Hill did not make him any wiser. *Most congressional representatives seem to have no interest in the historical events that put us in this situation,* he diarized days later.

When Saddam Hussein's Iraqi forces invaded Kuwait in August 1990, Troy decided he needed to do some research and document his best understanding of historical events that had led the nation to its continuous energy crisis. It took him a week to develop a document he titled *America's Achilles' Heel: The Oil Weapon.* The catchy title, thoroughness, and concise details began to get some attention on Capitol Hill. A copy of the eight-page publication sat prominently on many desks in Washington. And, in reaction to the publication, the U.S. Congress called for a full congressional inquiry into the issue of America's energy security and self-reliance. The White House enthusiastically supported it, and Troy was appointed to the panel.

"Congratulations, dear," Donna offered from San Diego when he told her of the appointment. "It's good to know your efforts are respected."

"Thanks." Troy forced a chuckle. "If more lobbyists knocking at my door is a sign of respect, I don't need it."

"Lobbyists?" Donna said.

Troy swallowed several times in an effort to relieve the choking feeling in his throat. "That's how it is around here. They're all over the place, and everyone seems scared stiff of the influence some of them have."

Donna felt dumbfounded but decided it was Troy's issue to resolve. "Don't compromise your own principles, honey. You could never live with that."

Troy smiled. "Thanks, dear." He kissed her over the telephone. "That's something mother would have said." He heard her kiss him back. "I love you."

It was a few months later. Troy had the cordless phone nestled in the crook of his neck and his feet propped up on his desk. "It had to be done," he explained to Donna, who was at the other end of the line in San Diego. "Saddam refused to comply with UN demands for his troops to leave Kuwait peacefully. We need to drive him out and end his war before things really get out of hand. If Cheney, Powell, and the Pentagon are as organized as I think they are, things will be over sooner rather than later."

"I hope you're right," Donna said. "How are things going with your Energy Committee?"

"That's on the back-burner until this Iraq issue is resolved."

Donna sensed he was tired. "It's late there, dear. I'm sure you're worn out. Get to bed." She made the sound of a kiss. "I love you."

If only I could get a good sleep, Troy thought. "Love you, dear. Give my love to Leslie and Jeff. I'll call you tomorrow night."

He pressed the off button, moved his feet from the desk to the floor, and put the telephone down. He leaned forward with his elbows on the desk and his forehead in the palms of his hands. *Dear Lord*, he thought, *please guide us in dealing with these Middle East problems. Protect the forces we're sending into harm's way.*

It was early spring 1991, not long after Iraqi forces were driven out of Kuwait by the decisive U.S. success in the Desert Storm War. Troy was in San Diego for a few days. He and Donna were sitting on the back patio of their home before dinner. They wore light jackets as protection against a cool breeze off the Pacific. Two glasses of iced tea were on the table, and they were discussing various challenges Washington was still facing.

"President Bush hopes to use the Desert Storm success as an entrée to a peace settlement between Israel and the Arab world,"

Troy explained. "But he's got a serious problem. The Arabs won't negotiate while Israel is constructing more settlements in the West Bank."

"Why are they still doing that?" Donna was honestly puzzled.

"A lot of us are asking the same thing," Troy answered. "Shamir says he needs to house thousands of Russian Jews who've been pouring into the Occupied Territories." He shrugged. "Unfortunately, Congress approved a $400-million loan guarantee and, despite President Bush's condition for that loan, Shamir intends to use it to finance the housing program."

"But—" She couldn't understand. "Why did Congress do that? To house Russian Jews?!"

Troy reached for his glass of iced tea. "I'm not sure many of us in Congress really know the full truth. I don't. It's unreal, the financial goodies squeezed out of Washington for Israel." He sipped his tea. "Israel's foreign minister promised to send a letter pledging that Israel won't settle any Russian Jews in the Occupied Territories, nor use the U.S. loan guarantee for that purpose. Hopefully, Bush can get Shamir to confirm it. Fact is, a lot of us are hoping Shamir and his Likud party lose in Israel's summer election."

A few months later, Donna was in Washington. It had been a warm summer day and the air conditioner was jacked-up in the apartment. It was getting late, there was an advertisement on the TV, and Troy seemed preoccupied.

"Something bothering you, dear?" she asked.

He turned his head and looked into her eyes. "Something I never realized before." He thought how best to phrase it. "The Jewish lobby visited my office today."

"And?" Donna asked after an awkward pause.

15

"That lobby never bothered with me before."

"Why now?"

Troy shrugged. "Rabin defeated Shamir in the election last month and everyone's optimistic about the coming peace talks. But we've got Jewish lobby groups in Washington insisting that we still need to give Israel those hundreds of millions of dollars to build settlements in Palestine for thousands of Russian Jews."

Donna recalled their previous discussions. "You thought our success in Desert Storm and the election of Yitzhak Rabin would—"

Troy nodded and cut her off. "I know. That's what I thought. But it's beginning to look like just the opposite. AIPAC is aggressively advocating—"

"Who's AIPAC?" Donna interrupted.

Troy thought for a moment, fitting the initials together. "It's the American Israel Public Affairs Committee; possibly one of the most powerful lobby organizations in Washington, along with the NRA. And there are others."

"I had no idea."

"I know, I know." Troy said. "It's still difficult for me to believe. It's often a non-stop thing in the corridors of Congress." There was an uncomfortable silence. "I did some research after they left my office." He felt energized by the opportunity to discuss his findings. "Both AIPAC and the Conference of Presidents of Major American Jewish Organizations were established back—" He paused to recall the date. "I think it was in 1957. AIPAC had a different name then; the American Zionist Council for Public Affairs. Its purpose has always been to support Israeli objectives within the United States, with focus on influencing public opinion and the collection of money for Israel."

Donna scratched an itch on her cheek as she looked into Troy's eyes. "You make it sound as if Israel's interests come ahead of—" She stopped herself.

Troy nodded. "I know. In fact, more than one senior government representative has suggested to me that Israel is America's fifty-first state, maybe the most important one."

"Jeez! Who'd ever say that?" Her voice gained force. "So, what did you say to AIPAC?"

Troy scratched his brow. "Not much. It was pretty clear to me that they don't care what I have to say."

Donna stared at him. "What did they tell you?" There was anger in her voice.

Troy cleared his throat. "It was about their showdown with President Bush. They're trying to line Congress up on Israel's side, the side of Shamir's Likud Israel. They want to force the president to provide that funding to settle the Russian Jews in the Occupied Territories."

Donna stood. "I feel sick! I'm going to bed."

During the weeks that followed, President Bush continued to delay granting the additional loan guarantees to Israel, and the Jewish American lobby organizations launched one of the most emotionally powerful lobbying and media campaigns ever before witnessed in Washington.

One evening, Troy and Donna were walking through the park near their Washington apartment. He looked at his watch. "President Bush is speaking on television in ten minutes. Let's head back."

They had settled into their easy chairs. The television was on CNN and President George H. W. Bush was well into his talk.

"Just months ago," the president said, "American men and women in uniform risked their lives to defend Israelis in the face of Iraqi Scud missiles, and indeed Desert Storm; while winning a war against aggression, also achieved the defeat of Israel's most dangerous adversary." He went on to describe that the White House was seeking peace between Israel and its Arab neighbours and that the peace process could be jeopardized if new Israeli settlements were constructed in the Occupied Territories.

Troy looked at Donna. "He's got to win re-election next year."

Donna shrugged. "I hope so."

A year later
September 1992; Washington

Donna loved Washington when the leaves were changing colour. The upcoming presidential election was the main topic of discussion in the city. It was late in the evening and they were propped up in bed, their backs against the pillows. Troy took the remote off the side table and clicked the television off, then threw the covers back, jumped out of bed, and started toward the bathroom.

"I don't like how the media seems to disregard so many of the achievements of the Bush Administration." He closed the bathroom door.

Donna had rearranged the pillows and seemed to be asleep when Troy returned. As he slid into bed and turned off the table lamp she mumbled, "I don't understand why there is so much fuss about Bill Clinton and the Democrats. Bush should be a shoo-in, shouldn't he? He straightened out Panama and drove Saddam Hussein out of Kuwait, the Cold War with Russia has ended, he won the standoff on the Israeli loan issue, and now it looks like he and Rabin can finally lead the world to peace in the Middle East."

Troy leaned over, kissed her, and wrapped his arm around her. "I agree. The president should win re-election, hands down." He closed his eyes. "But the media," he was almost asleep, "keeps harping on that *read my lips* thing."

"Is the media out to get him?"

"Some very powerful people in our country have great influence over—" he started snoring.

CHAPTER 2

SOUL MATES CHALLENGED

A month later

October 1992; Washington

It was 3:50 p.m. when the intercom buzzed on Troy's desk.

"Mr. Grumner is on the line, sir."

A rush of adrenalin. *Harry! Haven't spoken to him in over a year.* He picked up the receiver. "Harry, what a great surprise! Everything okay?"

"Hi, Troy." Harry chuckled. "Things are okay. I'm in Washington; in the building. Thought I'd drop around to see you, if you have a few moments."

"Can't wait!"

"Could be there in fifteen minutes, if it works with you."

"Coffee's ready."

Harry Grumner and Troy had been the closest of boyhood friends while growing up on acreages next to each other on the outskirts of Great Falls, Montana. Troy's father and mother had always lived in Great Falls. Harry's father and mother moved into the neighbouring sixty-acre plot from their home in Brooklyn with her

Grandpa Isaac within months of the Nazi rally at Madison Square Gardens on February 22, 1939. Both ladies were pregnant when Troy's father and two teenaged brothers went to war. They were all lost in battle. The ladies were in the same hospital room with their newborn sons in September 1944. Harry and Troy grew up almost as twins—always together, good athletes and teammates, competing respectfully for the best of grades in school. Troy's family was Catholic. Harry's father attended the same Catholic Church, but Harry always went with his mother and Grandpa Isaac to the Jewish Synagogue. Harry was named valedictorian of their grade twelve graduation class and obtained his economics and business degrees at Columbia University in New York a year after Troy graduated with his engineering degree from Butte University. When Troy and Donna married in the summer of 1965, Harry was Troy's best man. Troy was not able to attend Harry's wedding in Manhattan in 1966 and they had seen each other only a few times since then, but always exchanged cards on special occasions.

Troy was standing at his office door with his white shirt sleeves rolled up, tie loose, and collar button undone when Harry arrived. Harry was wearing a dark grey suit, white shirt, and black-striped tie. They shook hands and grabbed each other in bear hugs. When they stood back at arm's length, they said in unison, "You look great!" Except for their grey hair and slightly worn appearances, their eyes and facial expressions could have been mistaken for twin versions of Clark Gable and Tommy Lee Jones. Harry was about two inches shorter than Troy and heavier in stature. Both had lots of grey in their hair. Harry's hair was thick, parted on the right side, handsomely wavy and dishevelled, as if he'd been rubbing or scratching his head quite a bit. Troy had been to the barber earlier in the day and his hair looked neat in comparison.

"You haven't changed a bit," Harry laughed.

"You either, old buddy. Come on in."

Troy closed the door and motioned to the armchairs next to a low table set with two coffee mugs and a thermos. "There's fresh coffee, or there's a fifteen-year scotch in the cabinet."

"You're still good at option plays," Harry joked, looking at his watch. "It's past five somewhere. Option two for me, please. I need it."

Troy brought an unopened bottle of fifteen-year, single-malt scotch, two glasses, and a small bucket of ice back to the table. He cracked the bottle and poured a couple of ounces into each glass. "Ice or water?"

"This looks perfect to me." Harry grabbed his glass and held it out to Troy. "To old times."

Their glasses clicked. "To old times." Troy leaned over and added a couple of ice cubes to his glass.

They gave the scotch time to work its heat past their throats before their eyes fixed on each other.

"Thanks for coming by, Harry. I wasn't aware you were in the building."

"Don't get to Washington much. Never been inside this Capitol Building before." Harry loosened his tie and undid the collar button.

"You're still an exec at Citibank?"

"Left the bank last year. Been focused on fundraising in New York State since then."

"Don't remember you mentioning that in your note at Christmas," Troy said. "Democrats?" He reached for his glass.

"Ya," Harry laughed.

"Well, ol' buddy, I hope you're not after *my* money!"

"Wouldn't give it a thought." Harry rubbed his head. "But I need to discuss something else with you."

Troy wanted to catch up on Harry's family situation. "It's been a while since you and I touched base, other than our notes last Christmas. Last time we saw each other was after you and Rebecca returned from your second trip to Israel. Are the boys on their own now?"

For half an hour, they discussed their families and some of their interesting adventures. Several times Harry attempted to change the subject and get to the real reason for his visit, but Troy kept the topic centred on their families. Harry and Rebecca were working toward full retirement. Their oldest son, David, was a trauma surgeon in Brooklyn. Jacob, the younger, had a medical degree, was just completing an engineering degree in medical instrumentation, and would be joining a research team at Scripps after graduation in a few months.

"Scripps? In San Diego?" Troy asked.

"Uh-huh, in La Jolla, I think." Harry stood up, took off his jacket, and flopped it over the back of his chair.

"That's near where we live. It's part of my constituency. Jeff works for Scripps."

"You're kidding!" Harry was rolling back his shirtsleeves.

"I want Jacob to call us."

"For sure."

"You've got my number at the house, haven't you?"

"Yep, somewhere."

They emptied their glasses and Troy poured more. "So, what's on your mind, Harry?"

Harry sipped the scotch, suddenly sensitive to the message he'd been sent to deliver. "I understand you're on a congressional committee that's charged with assessing U.S. energy issues. How's that going?" It was a diversion.

"Pretty slow right now. It got started with some research I did in an effort to understand our obsession with Middle East oil."

"I've heard a few people were quite surprised by the report."

"Maybe. I titled it *America's Achilles' Heel, The Oil Weapon*. It was probably that title that created most of the reaction here on Capitol Hill." He shrugged off the importance of his appointment. "You're probably aware that congressional committees are a dime a dozen."

"Congratulations, anyway. Knowing you, I'm sure it was a thorough report."

"I kept getting deeper and deeper into it," Troy said. "It's still hard for me to believe our country was the largest oil producer and exporter in the world until the late forties."

"What happened?"

"When World War Two ended, Roosevelt and Churchill were determined to keep Russia from gaining control of Middle East oil and they pushed our major oil companies to redirect much of their focus there. It got us militarily involved in Iran, prompted the Suez Canal crisis in 1956, and the beginning of OPEC in 1957. The real shock for American oil companies came in the late sixties when President Johnson removed the import quota system that was designed to protect a portion of our market for domestic oil producers."

Harry tipped his glass for the last drop.

"Here." Troy grabbed the bottle, added another couple of ounces to each glass.

25

"Then there was the Six-Day War in June '67. And, when Washington and the Brits wouldn't support the UN in condemning Israel's attack, OPEC countries stopped oil sales to us. Thankfully, that time, there was excess production capacity in the rest of the world and we were able to cover our oil requirements from elsewhere."

"I don't remember any of that," Harry said. "I thought their oil weapon—"

"That came later," Troy interrupted, "after the Yom Kippur War in 1973. But before that, a few critical things happened. U.S. domestic production declined when it couldn't compete with the cheaper imports, our inflation rate went sky-high, and the Arab nations were angry because of our perceived support of Israel's persistent push into the Occupied Territories. When they heard Washington planned to send Phantom and Skyhawk fighter jets to Israel, the Arabs began to panic. And the Soviet's weren't sleeping. They made an anti-Zionist pact with Iraq."

"I've never heard it described in that context." Harry sipped his scotch.

"It got worse," Troy continued. "In September '72, Black September terrorists killed eleven Israeli Olympic Team members in Munich and Israel retaliated by bombing Palestinian refugee locations in Lebanon and Syria. Then, early the next year, Israeli jets shot down a Libyan Arab Airlines passenger plane and killed more than a hundred civilians. We used our veto power in the Security Council to prevent UN efforts to halt Israeli aggressions. I'm sure you know as much as I do about the Yom Kippur War in October '73. The Arabs' Oil Weapon followed that war."

"I was in New York," Harry said. "Everyone was happy as hell that America saved Israel in that war, but we really suffered during the energy crisis. It seemed to last forever. We couldn't drive our cars, couldn't take elevators, couldn't wash in warm water or heat our homes properly. It was a disaster!"

"I know." Troy shrugged. "I think we're in danger of heading in the same direction again."

"What!" Harry sat forward, hands on his knees, staring at Troy.

"We need to be more careful how we handle Middle East issues. Bush is trying to—" Troy stopped himself. "Anyway, that's the background behind our energy committee. Let's get to what's on your mind."

There was a long pause. Harry rubbed both hands through his hair and looked into Troy's eyes.

"There's pressure on us, on all American Jewry, to encourage President Bush to release that $400-million loan to Israel uncondi- tionally. If he won't—" He stopped when he saw Troy's face go white. "Most Jews in America respect the Bush presidency and what it has accomplished. But we've got to stick together."

There was a long silence. They each had their glass at their mouths but the scotch simply touched lips without being swallowed.

Troy broke the silence. "Harry," he shook his head, "I can't believe you said that after the story I just told!" He didn't give Harry a chance to speak. "I should tell you another one." He swallowed to relieve a choked feeling in his throat. "I'd been here in Washington about a year when one of the old boys in the House cornered me. He'd been on the Hill for many years and had seen a lot. He was a year from retirement. A really highly respected guy. I guess he'd taken a shine to me and wanted to make sure his experience, efforts, knowledge, and hopes weren't totally forgotten. He was Jewish. He made it clear that one of his greatest disappointments and concerns was the growing

27

power and influence of Zionist lobbies in our federal and state governments and the media." Troy paused to clear his throat. "At that point, I didn't really have a clear idea what he was talking about. Anyway, he pointed out that those pressures had increased dramatically since the Six Day War in 1967. He thought that military success had created a newfound confidence, machoism, and outspokenness among a lot of Jewish Americans, as if each last one of them had participated as victorious warriors. He was afraid that emotional connection had, over the years, along with the Yom Kippur War, somehow tied a Zionist noose around the necks of all American Jews. He pointed out how, during his time in Washington, he had felt forced to approve federal programs that would end up transferring trillions of America's dollars to Israel through tax-free charities, tax-deductible donations, forgivable loans; stuff like that. He hoped the Bush Administration would try to halt it all by standing up—"

"I understand what you're saying," Harry interrupted, "although I'm surprised he volunteered all—"

"He clearly needed to get it off his chest, as an American."

"But religious groups and their lobbies are fundamental to what America stands for, Troy." Harry cleared his throat and quoted as best he could, "No laws will prohibit the free exercise of religion or abridge freedom of speech or of the press, or the right of people peaceably to assemble, and to petition the government for a redress of grievances."

Troy breathed deeply, twice, in an effort to relieve his sudden anxiety. "I'm impressed with your memory, Harry. Well done." He took another deep breath. "But I don't believe the First Amendment intended to encourage lobbyists to control our governments, certainly not when lobbying for other nations!" He got up, walked to his desk, hit the intercom, and told his secretary she could leave for the evening. When he settled back into his chair, his chin and mouth were tight with determination and his eyes looked like he was ready to fight.

Harry looked at his watch. "I've got a dinner appointment at—"

"Cancel that," Troy said. "There are things we should discuss. I'll order in some pizza." He looked into Harry's eyes. "Okay?"

After some hesitation, Harry made a telephone call to cancel his dinner obligation, and Troy ordered a pizza with Caesar salad from the best Italian take-out restaurant in Washington. They started drinking coffee. The Bush–Israel issue was dropped for the time being as they discussed the pros and cons of the European Union. Then the food arrived. Troy put the pizza and salad in the centre of the table and took china dinner plates, cutlery, and paper napkins out of one of his cabinets.

"You've got quite the setup here," Harry laughed.

"Need to; I'm working most nights." He walked to the far corner of the room and opened the cooler. "White or red wine?"

"I'll stick with coffee. Some water would be good."

Troy placed two bottles of cold water on the table and poured more coffee. They loaded their plates and started eating.

"Great pizza," Harry offered.

"My favourite take-out." Troy had another mouthful before asking, "Do you miss the banking?"

Harry shrugged. "Not really. The industry just got too central-ized and top-heavy for me to enjoy. When I started back in the sixties, there were a lot of independent regional banks focused on local markets. But the big guys, the big banks with international owners and bosses, have taken over most of those banks. The bro-kerage, investment, and insurance businesses, too. They're dictating

29

most all operating policies now." He paused and sipped his coffee. "I often wonder why Washington let all that centralization happen, because antitrust laws used to focus on limiting the concentration of Wall Street, the banks, and insurance power."

"Just another example of powerful lobbyists in Washington," Troy said. "We just don't seem to have the guts to hold firm against self-serving businesses and lobbyists who don't really care about the long-term integrity and liveability of our country."

Harry nodded. "Frankly, Troy, I'm feeling kind of embarrassed about having brought the subject of the Israeli loan into your office."

Troy nodded, indicating he understood his old friend's apology. "That old House member I told you about was determined our only focus here should be toward the long-term safety and pleasure of Americans in this country. He believed the UN was meant to support our focus toward other nations, and that international corporations needed to be closely watched by Washington. And, talking about events in Israel, he believed the UN needed to take up residence there until there's an internationally sanctioned agreement and things are operating peacefully."

"That may never—"

"He was sure world Zionists would never agree to that. I told him that I didn't really understand who the world Zionists are. He explained that, as far as he knew, that movement didn't exist with much political significance until late in the nineteenth century. He said it was led by powerful bankers in Europe, headed by the Rothschild family, and became focused in the early nineteen hundreds on persuading the British government to establish a Jewish homeland. He seemed convinced that most Jews were not supportive of that initiative because, except maybe for the Jews in Russia, they had already established their own homelands." Troy took a deep breath. "He could get pretty damn emotional about that whole subject, and was convinced the movement had just become too secretly and disproportionately powerful in America."

Harry nodded. "If Grandpa Isaac were still alive, he might agree with that." A picture of him and his mother standing at Grandpa Isaac's deathbed when he was a young lad in Great Falls flashed into Harry's mind and he recalled the old man's warning: *They convinced Britain to create a homeland for us in Israel, but our homeland is America! Their homeland idea will smother us. World Zionists will use our people for their own purpose, and Harry there won't be able to do much of anything without their blessing."* The image left Harry's mind. "But," he cleared his throat, "we intuitively sense we must stick together. Anti-Semitism is so prevalent. We just can't afford to let outsiders see even the slightest internal conflict among us." He shrugged at the inevitability. "It's just part of who we are. You know what I'm saying, don't you, Troy?"

Troy nodded. "I might, especially after my years here in Washington. But," he paused, "I think that old House representative had a much deeper commitment to his own country and his congressional responsibilities than to any agenda important to Israel or wealthy foreign bankers."

Harry nodded. "I'm sure you're right, and good for him on that score."

They were on the third slices of pizza. Each knew more was to be said. Finally, Troy spoke.

"Harry, you came to my office at the beckoning of a powerful network of lobbyists, hoping to convince me to participate with a gang in Congress to put pressure on President Bush. Did you really

31

think there was any chance I'd embrace the idea?" His voice was getting too loud and he swallowed hard before continuing more quietly. "Don't American Jews need to stop being the workhorse for a Zionist network that uses Israel as its call to arms?" Immediately, he wished it had come out different.

Harry took it as a personal insult. He quickly stood. *Don't talk to me like that, old buddy. Fuck you!* he thought. "I need to go," he said instead. "Can you call me a cab?"

An awkward silence followed and nothing more was said until they walked out the side door to the waiting taxi. Harry turned to Troy and extended his hand.

"It's been great seeing you again, Troy." Their grips were solid and each had trouble releasing, as if they might never see each other again.

Troy forced a smile. "Thanks for coming. I'm sorry I got carried away back there." He paused. "We'll look forward to seeing Jacob when he gets to La Jolla."

Harry just nodded, turned, and got into the back seat of the waiting taxi. As the car pulled away, Troy started walking back to the building with his chin down in regret. He tried to console himself as he closed the door and started down the corridor to his office. *Harry knows it wasn't personal.* He hadn't gone far before his mind suddenly filled with pictures of the lobbyists who would be walking the same corridors the next morning. His stomach turned.

CHAPTER 3

DOOMED PEACE TALKS

A few weeks later
November 4, 1992; Washington

"I still can't believe what happened," Donna mumbled.

She and Troy were in the den of their Washington apartment eating chicken stir-fry dinners off TV tables and watching the eight o'clock news. All news channels were giving their listeners independent survey assessments of the presidential election the previous evening. Their channel was set on *TST NEWS*.

"Exit polls from yesterday's election indicate female and Jewish voters overwhelmingly supported Bill Clinton," the moderator explained as he turned to one of his two guests. "Do you believe that?"

"I'm a bit surprised," the guest answered. "But the media's had President Bush in its sights for over a year. You know, first there was the Israeli loan controversy and then, after Rabin defeated Shamir, the media shifted focus to that read-my-lips issue."

The moderator and camera swung to the second guest. "I agree, most of our American media was clearly in Clinton's camp," she offered. "That was the difference."

Troy grabbed the remote and turned the volume almost off.

"I still can't believe President Bush lost," Donna repeated.

Troy shrugged. "We can't cry over spilt milk. The question now is whether or not Clinton will keep pressure on the Palestinian peace process. I think he's got two willing negotiators in Rabin and Arafat."

Donna stood and collected the plates. "Finish your wine, honey. I'll get the dessert and coffee."

As he waited for Donna to return, Troy wondered, *What else is on Clinton's plate? NAFTA is finalized. Noriega's out of control in Panama. Bombing will likely continue against Iraq. Clinton's got to get Rabin and Arafat to sign a peace accord.* Nothing else came quickly to his mind, and a second later Donna returned from the kitchen with her hands full.

Two years later
Late 1995; Washington

Troy and Donna were in the den watching TST's evening coverage of Prime Minister Rabin's assassination by an Israeli terrorist.

"He was a fine leader," Troy remarked.

"I'll never understand what goes on over there." Donna wanted to change the subject. "Have you told Harry how much we enjoyed having Jacob to dinner last month?"

"Not yet." He had never told her about his embarrassing insult of his old pal or the fact they had not spoken to each other in a couple of years. *I should call him.*

Donna grabbed the remote, turned the TV off, and finished her wine. "I'm tired."

"Me too." Troy finished his wine. "I've got a busy day of meetings tomorrow."

Many leaders in Washington were sensing that another oil crisis was in the making, and they looked to Troy as one with knowledge and connections with the international oil industry. It was a cold day in early December when top executives from two of the nation's major international oil companies visited Troy's office on the hill. Troy knew each of them well and they got right to business.

"If Peres loses Israel's upcoming election to the Likud, it will likely kill the Oslo Accord," Troy said. "Could that drop us right back to the mid-seventies as far as oil security is concerned?"

"I understand what you mean," the elderly executive said. "Rabin's assassination shocked us all. The Arabs had come to trust Rabin, and I think they trust Peres. For now, our supply lines are secure." He paused. "But we're importing more now than we imported at the peak of the energy crisis in the seventies. It's important that Peres move Rabin's peace agenda along, quickly. If terrorist elements ever—"

"Are your operations protected against terrorist attacks?" Troy said.

"Not really. Our operations are so widespread—oil fields, pipelines, ocean tankers, refineries, distribution networks—it's impossible to cover everything."

Troy had heard the same story from others. "What's your assessment of the peace process?"

"It's critically important. If Peres and his Labour party maintain power in Israel, there's a chance." The other executive nodded agreement and added, "But if Likud gets back in, all bets are off."

That night, Troy had a restless sleep. The first call he made from his office the next morning was to Harry Grumner in New York.

"Hello, Harry. Hope you're well."

"Things are fine here. I've been meaning to send you a note of thanks for the way your whole family has welcomed Jacob to the west coast. We really appreciate that."

"He's a good man. A chip off the old block. Reminds me a lot of you. I'm glad he's doing so well." Troy paused. "I need your thoughts and advice on something."

"What is it?"

"What's your sense of the support for the Oslo Accord? Is Peres going to retain power?"

It took a moment for Harry to answer. "Likud's determined to beat Labour in the June election. If that happens, Netanyahu will likely reject the accord immediately." He paused. "It's not what I'd like to see, but I think it might be a foregone conclusion. Likud and the settlers in the Territories do not support Labour's peace initiatives."

"Not very encouraging," Troy said.

"I know." Harry paused. "Don't tell anyone I said this to you, but I think the only way the accord can work is if the UN is in there to administer all the territories for a long time and can keep peace until there's an agreement and everything settles down. I'm sensing that international money is prepared to rush into that area if that happened."

"Really? Interesting! Would the Knesset agree to UN involvement?"

"Probably not without strong Washington insistence." Harry coughed. "Do you think Congress would do that?"

"Not likely. Not as long as we let lobbyists roam our corridors." Troy took a deep breath and cleared his dry throat. "I've got to go, Harry. Thanks for your thoughts. Please give me a call if you come up with any new ideas."

"Don't hold your breath. Thanks for calling."

In June 1996, Benjamin Netanyahu's Likud party defeated Shimon Peres' Labour party, largely because of overwhelming support from the immigrant settlers in the Occupied Territories. President Clinton's White House administration was determined to bring Prime Minister Netanyahu and Yasser Arafat to the negotiating table. Troy and Harry were communicating quite regularly as events unfolded.

"It's hopeless," Harry said during a discussion in mid-1997. "Like we've agreed before, it will only happen with direct UN involvement right on the ground in Israel and Palestine; maybe even economic sanctions should be applied to force things along."

"Congress will never agree to sanctions against Israel."

"I know. I've got to go. Talk to you in a few weeks."

It was a year later. Troy slammed the front door after entering his Washington apartment. Donna was in the kitchen preparing dinner. He walked into the kitchen with his suitcoat over his arm, his tie and the top button of his white shirt undone. Donna looked as beautiful as ever. He gave her a hug and kiss.

"You look weary." There was a quizzical tone in her voice.

"One of the worst days I've had on the Hill!" He shook his head in disgust as he tossed his coat over the back of a chair. "Can't believe I'm involved with such a group of idiots." He sat down and rested his forearms on the table. "The House passed a resolution today backing Jerusalem as Israel's undivided capital." He slapped both palms down. "Idiots! Do you know what that means?" He didn't wait for her to answer. "It means we have just told all Muslim nations that, as far as Washington is concerned, the Likud's in control of East Jerusalem and the Dome on the Rock."

"Why would Congress do that?"

"Lobby pressures again. This time Christian fundamentalists have joined in with the Zionists! Shit!"

Donna continued to busy herself at the sink.

In October 1998, a Clinton-sponsored negotiation between Netanyahu and Arafat finally resulted in the Wye Peace Agreement. However, few world leaders were optimistic or enthusiastic, and most were not surprised when it unravelled. But Clinton's White House administration was determined. Following Ehud Barak's Labour party's defeat of Netanyahu's Likud party, President Clinton sponsored peace talks between Barak and Arafat at the Camp David retreat in the spring and summer of 2000.

Troy and Donna were lunching on the back patio of their San Diego home on July 28, 2000.

"Jeff is bringing Jacob Grumner for dinner on Sunday," Donna said.

"Good." Troy seemed only partially interested.

"Something bothering you?" Donna asked.

Troy said nothing for several minutes as he focused on the chirping birds flitting from limb to limb in the dense trees at the back of their property. "The Camp David peace talks have failed." He shrugged. "I'm not really surprised. Arafat's got to be a frustrating man to deal with, but I can't believe Clinton indicated he's thinking of shifting our embassy from Tel Aviv to Jerusalem. Hope it's just a pressure tactic."

"Do you think Barak will win re-election in Israel?"

Troy shook his head. "It's hard to tell. If Ariel Sharon wins the Likud leadership from Netanyahu, watch out!"

Donna stood and started to collect the empty plates. "It's quite a coincidence, isn't it? Elections both here and in Israel, right at the beginning of the twenty-first century. Right when many fundamentalists are preaching Armageddon is about to happen!"

"It's more than interesting," Troy said. "It's scary!"

Sunday was a beautiful day. Troy was relaxing on the back patio when Jeff and Jacob arrived at 3:30. The boys walked out to the patio with three mugs of beer.

"Thought you'd like one of these, Dad."

"Thanks." Troy took his mug from Jeff and turned to Jacob. "How are you, Jacob?" he asked. *You're the spitting image of your dad,* he thought.

"I'm fine, thank you, Mr. Rogers. You look well. Dad asked me to extend his hello and best wishes."

The boys sat down. They all lifted and touched their mugs together. The only other sounds came from the chirping birds in the trees at the back of the yard.

Troy turned to Jacob. "Your folks are well?"

"They are. I haven't seen them in two months, but we're on the phone at least once a week." He looked into Troy's eyes. "Last time I spoke with Dad, he mentioned you're both quite concerned about the lack of progress with the Middle East peace talks."

Troy nodded, not sure it was a good time to discuss the subject. "We both consider it to be a very serious problem."

"I agree," Jacob said. "Hard for me to believe it's been going on for so long." It was clearly something he wanted to discuss. "Dad thinks the United Nations needs to be directly involved. It all started so long ago! I think—," he paused to grab his mug, "really, it's something I'm just not able to properly understand." He took a couple of swigs.

"Me too," Jeff said, before sipping his beer in the sudden silence. He finally offered, "Makes no sense to me why, over so many years, the UN hasn't been able to just take control of things. Shouldn't UN forces just go in there and peacefully police a lasting settlement?"

"I think Dad would agree with that," Jacob reacted. "He feels, if that were to happen, the whole Middle East would probably become the most productive economy in the world." He shrugged. "But I think he also expects Israel will probably never let it happen."

"Why not?" Jeff asked.

Troy felt like saying something but decided to let the younger generation play it out.

Jacob looked at Troy, then back to Jeff. "I think Dad would say that sometimes we Jews have trouble sharing things with others. He calls it our leaders' protocol, whatever that means!" His eyes focused into his mug as he tipped it to his mouth.

Jeff looked at his dad. Troy shrugged and reached for his beer.

"Dad would probably say that's just how it is," Jacob continued, "until the leaders of Israel are completely convinced there's a better way for them."

Troy wanted to change the subject. "I'm glad you two have become good friends." He slugged down the last of his beer and slid his glass across the table toward Jeff. "How about another beer? And let's gets some bets down on who's going to be in the World Series this fall."

Jacob jumped up from his seat and slapped Jeff on the shoulder. "I'm ready for another one too, buddy."

Troy watched the two of them as they walked side-by-side across the patio toward the back door of the house. *Just like Harry and I used to be*, he thought.

It was four months later, the fall of 2000. The outgoing Clinton White House administration was in a panic over the likelihood of another energy crisis. Equally concerning was the realization there would not be an early Middle East peace settlement. Vice-President Al Gore, who was the Democratic Party's choice to run for president in the November election, turned his focus to the country's strategic oil reserve in an effort to take pressure off domestic oil supply and prices.

In early October, Yasser Arafat pleaded with the United Nations to speak out against what he called the "Israeli killing machine." During a debate between the two U.S. presidential candidates on October 11, both Gore and the Republican's George W. Bush indicated strong support for Israel and rebuffed Arafat's plea. On October 19, 2000, the United Nations accused Israel of war crimes and human rights violations; Israel and the United States were the only countries opposed to the UN resolution.

The November 7 U.S. presidential election was too close to call. It took weeks before a winner was declared, and the Clinton White House administration seemed paralyzed in dealing with Middle East issues. On December 13, Al Gore conceded the U.S. presidency to George W. Bush.

"Why did he do it?" Donna asked Troy as they spoke on the telephone that evening.

Troy was in the study of his Washington apartment. "I'm not sure. Maybe he decided we'd better get on with the affairs of state. There are some very serious things we need to deal with."

Donna sensed concern in his voice. "Anything new?"

He was not at liberty to tell her about new top-secret security concerns that had been privately circulating in Washington ever since the bombing of the *USS Cole* while it was in harbour off the Yemen coast on October 12. "Right now, everything depends on Middle East peace," he answered.

President Clinton made one final effort to bring Arafat and Barak to a common ground. On December 22, 2000, a peace proposal was presented calling for 1) establishment of a demilitarized Palestinian state in all of the Gaza Strip and ninety-six per cent of the West Bank, including parts of the Old City of Jerusalem, 2) an Israeli security presence along the Jordan Valley for six years, 3) Palestinian sovereignty over the Al-Aksa mosque compound, with Israel to have control of the archaeological sites that lie beneath the surface, Palestinians to have control of traditional Arab neighbourhoods of Jerusalem, and 4) Palestinians to scale back their demanded right of return of Palestinian refugees. The proposal failed.

Troy flew to San Diego in mid-December 2000 and planned to be at home for the next forty-five days.

Christmas Day had always been a special time in the Rogers family. This was no exception. The outside of the house and several trees in the yard were decorated with lights. Wrapped gifts were under a large decorated Christmas tree in the corner of the family room. Christmas morning, Donna prepared the turkey, Troy helped her get it into the oven, and they had a light breakfast of fruit and cereal. The kids and their families arrived about two o'clock in the afternoon. Leslie and her husband, Tim, were expecting their first child. Jeff, thirty, was engaged to his high school sweetheart, Colleen. By mid-afternoon, they were opening gifts in the family room. After all the gifts and wrappings had been cleared from that room, Donna and the two girls set the dining-room table and worked in the kitchen while the boys gathered in the den to watch television.

"Dad, what do you think will happen when George W. Bush takes over the White House?" Tim asked.

Troy thought for a couple of seconds before answering. "I had a deep respect for his father when he was president. If George two is anything like his father, I think America has some good years ahead."

They talked about various aspects of Washington politics until Donna called, "Dear, come and carve the turkey."

Early February 2001; Washington

On February 6, 2001, two weeks after George W. Bush was sworn in as the forty-third president of the United States, Ariel Sharon won a landslide victory over Ehud Barak for the leadership of Israel.

Troy had spent the day in meetings with various Israeli analysts, trying to get some idea of what actions Israel might take under Sharon's leadership. He and Harry Grumner also had a long talk on the telephone. As he readied for bed that night, one point that Harry made kept running through Troy's mind: *Everywhere Sharon has gone, trouble has followed.* Troy flung his white shirt into the laundry basket and undid his belt. *The butchery in Lebanon when he was Israel's defence minister in the eighties—that started the First Palestinian Intifada,* Harry had reminded him. He hung up his pants and sat in the chair by the bed to take off his socks. *And in the early nineties, when he was housing minister, Israel ploughed down*

Palestinian orchards and villages to construct illegal settlements for Jewish immigrants from Russia. He threw the socks into the basket. *And the march he led to the Temple Mount last year started the Second Intifada.* Troy took a deep breath and dropped back on the bed with his head on a pillow. He closed his eyes, wishing he could roll over and hug Donna, but she was home in San Diego. *When George Sr. was president, he tried to keep the Likud in check.* Troy's legs twitched involuntarily. *I hope George W. follows in his father's footsteps and is more successful.* He burped and choked on the bile that rose to his throat.

On May 13, 2001, the secretary-general of the United Nations accused Israel of excessive force in its battle against Palestinians. He indicated Israel should be using proper crowd control methods rather than rifles and mortar shells. On May 17, the UN Security Council condemned Israel's continuing actions against Palestinians, especially concerned about the persistent deterioration of the political, social and economic situations in the region, and the fact that closures and other measures imposed by Israeli authorities were preventing UN field staff and emergency relief deliveries from getting to many areas of Palestine. A follow-up UN commission report called for urgent measures to remove Israeli restrictions placed on the movement of agency staff and goods in keeping with international law.

Troy was beginning to have mixed feeling about the new Bush White House. At times, he felt President Bush was a chip off the old block, and at other times he sensed the president had no idea what his vice-president, secretary of defence, and secretary of state were doing. And representatives on his Energy Committee were beginning to express similar feelings.

Troy called Harry in New York after Ariel Sharon's visit to Washington in early June. He quickly got to the point. "What's your reaction to Sharon's announcement that Israel will accept the idea of peace with Palestinians only after a prolonged cease fire and will not stop construction of new settlements in the occupied territories?"

"Didn't really surprise me," Harry reacted. There was an awkward silence before he continued. "You know, Troy, I think if they were still alive, both my father and Grandpa Isaac would have a clear and serious message for American leaders right now."

"What's that?"

It took Harry a few seconds to answer. "America gained a great deal by staying out of it while the Nazi military marched through most of mainland Europe in the late nineteen-thirties," another awkward pause, "but America could very easily end up paying a great price for watching Zionists do much the same thing in Palestine today."

On July 1, 2001, Israeli warplanes struck military posts in Syria and Lebanon, breaking existing peace agreements with those nations. In protest against Prime Minister Sharon's actions, Shimon Peres, the leader of Israel's Labour Party, resigned from Sharon's cabinet, and the White House condemned Israel's actions.

A couple of months later, Troy and Donna were sitting in the den of their Washington apartment watching the TST evening news. When the news ended, Troy turned to Donna, not sure if he should tell her what had been tugging on his mind for the past couple of months. Then it came out.

"It seems to me all the unsuccessful peace talks we've sponsored for more than a decade have really just been a bunch of fabricated tactics. I hate feeling negative like this. When that happens to me, it's a clear sign."

Donna turned to him. "What did I miss? What are you talking about?"

He shrugged. "This feeling's been building in me. I don't think I belong here in Washington anymore. It's impossible for me to have an impact. Partisanship, lobbyists, and the media are all that's running our country now. Along with the White House administration, they have us all looking like fools." He took a deep breath. "I should get out of Washington as soon as I can."

Donna could hardly believe her ears. She struggled to control her emotions. "Want to talk about it?"

"Since George W. and his gang moved into the White House things have—" he paused, searching for specifics. "Their unilateral actions regarding the defence shield and the Kyoto Accord, the arrogant approach toward the Chinese after our spy plane went down over there, and other things. Arrogance of any kind does not sit well with me—you know that. Congress and the White House should be working together, not battling each other on everything. And feeling like we're in Israel's pocket is a total insult. It's not right, not for the America I love and believe in. I don't think I should stick around here when I feel this way."

Donna had seen the same moral determination and commitment in Troy before and had always respected his choices. "I understand," she said. "Whatever you decide, you know the whole family will support you."

"I know, honey." Troy stood, leaned over, and kissed her on the forehead. "You go home tomorrow. I'll follow in a few days. I can't stand being here longer than I have to be." He kissed her again. "I love you." He stretched to ease his anxiety, walked into the kitchen, took a bottle of water from the refrigerator, and had it half drank by the time he got back to the den. *I need to leave Washington. Not sure what I'd do. Maybe become a lobbyist; they really haul in the bucks. Or maybe do some writing.*

CHAPTER 4

DISASTER STRIKES

Eight days later
September 11, 2001

The American Airlines Boeing 767, Flight 11, left Boston Airport at 7:45 a.m. with ninety-two people aboard. Thirteen minutes later, United Airlines Boeing 757, Flight 175, left the same airport with sixty-five aboard. Both flights were scheduled to fly across the continent to Los Angeles, California. At 8:01 a.m., United Airlines Boeing 757, Flight 93, with forty-five people aboard, left Newark, New Jersey, for San Francisco, and, at 8:10 a.m., an American Airlines Boeing 757, Flight 77, left Washington for Los Angeles with sixty-four people aboard.

Also at 8:10 a.m., Flight 11 plowed into the north tower of the World Trade Center in New York City. Fifty-five minutes later, Flight 175 plowed into the south tower. Both towers were 110 stories high, the tallest office towers in North America. At 9:58 a.m., the south tower of the World Trade Center collapsed and the north tower followed it to a grave of twisted steel and ashy rubble at 10:28 a.m. At 9:39 a.m., Flight 77 plowed into the Pentagon, and, at 10:10 a.m., Flight 93 crashed near Shanksville, Pennsylvania, after heroic passengers prevented the terrorists from reaching the intended crash site in Washington.

The same morning
San Diego, California

Troy had arrived home from Washington late the previous night. He and Donna had talked and made love. He carefully rolled out of bed and walked across the plush bedroom carpet toward the bathroom, feeling the warmth on his feet and ankles as he walked over the short patch of carpet hit by the bright morning sun coming through the east window. His biceps flexed as he used the fingers of both hands to rub the stiffness at the back of his neck. His greyed hair was dishevelled. The muscular shape of his naked body belied his fifty-nine years. As he reached for the doorknob, he yawned and stifled the tendency to vocalize so not to wake Donna. Twenty minutes later, he opened the bathroom door. His hair was still damp and uncombed.

"Time to rise and shine, honey." He bent over and kissed Donna on the ear.

"Mmmm," she turned and looked up at him. "You smell good."

He kissed her on the lips.

"I love kissing you right after you shave." She smiled slyly. "You want to play?"

He slid under the covers.

She threw the covers back. "Let me run to the bathroom first."

He patted her bottom as she rolled out her side of the bed. "Hurry back." Watching her walk across the room he thought, *She keeps herself in such good shape. I'm a lucky guy, and so glad to be home.*

"Wow," Donna exclaimed thirty minutes later. She rolled to the edge of the bed and grabbed her nightgown off a chair. "I'll put the coffee on."

Ten minutes later, Troy was doing up his belt when Donna screamed.

"Troy!" She screamed louder. "Troy! My God, come here! Quick, Troy!" Her voice cracked. Troy hurried toward the bedroom door as Donna screamed again. "Troy! Troy! My God!"

At 11:00 p.m. that night, they were still flipping television channels, trying to pick up any new information they could, as the worst attack in history against the mainland of the United States continued to play out on the nation's television news channels. The news was irritatingly repetitive; nothing new, nothing good, the death toll and injured changing by the minute and without any hope of knowing the final result for days. Donna flipped the channel to the TST network.

"And now, for the latest reactions from people on the streets of Manhattan, here is Carol Fulton reporting directly from Times Square." The picture wasn't clear, as if the cameraman had given one quick swipe across an ash-covered camera lens just before going on the air. Carol Fulton, TST's most popular news anchor, was standing at the south end of Times Square with a microphone at her mouth, blinking repeatedly in an effort to keep her eyes moist in the cloudy, pungent, particle-laden air. People were rushing in different directions, others moving slowly or not at all, and most looking baffled and numb. The only eyes that turned toward Carol and her cameraman were sad, discouraged, or angry, and those quickly turned away as Carol tried to catch them for an interview.

"Authorities report that our first responders have taken control of lower Manhattan." Carol's clothes, hair, and eyebrows were grey with ash. "Many things are still unknown. Clean-up will take weeks, maybe months. There are no guesses as to how long it will take Manhattan to recover from the devastation. The FBI and New York police believe there is no reason to fear any future immediate acts of violence."

A small middle-aged woman passed nearby, clutching her husband's right shirtsleeve with both her hands. "Excuse me," Carol said. "Can you—?"

"This is unbelievable," the lady shouted in a weak and trembling voice.

"What the hell's wrong with our security here in America?" her husband shouted as they kept walking.

"Nuke the bastard Arabs!" shouted an old man on her right.

"We're paying for our idiotic policies in the Middle East!" shouted someone on her other side.

Troy shook his head. "This is a waste of time." He clicked the TV off. "Let's go to bed, honey. Nothing we can do to change what's going to happen over the next few days."

"We can just be thankful our family is safe," Donna offered as she stood with a weary sigh.

"I'll try to contact Harry again tomorrow," Troy said as they left the room. "We can only hope and pray he and his family are safe."

Three days later
San Diego

It was 8:30 a.m. Security at the San Diego airport was irritatingly tight.

"Sorry I can't see you to the gate, dear." Donna's cheeks were flushed and hollow as she tried to smile. They had left the house early and she had no make-up.

Troy looked into her eyes. "Everything's going to be okay. This extra security is necessary. It's good. We'll get things under control." His voice lacked the usual conviction.

"I love you, dear." She felt like she was sending him off to war as she threw her arms around his neck.

Troy held her close, saying nothing. Finally, he relaxed his arms, stepped back, and looked into her eyes. "Everything will be okay, honey," he repeated. "Don't worry. We'll get on top of this." He squeezed her arm lovingly and kissed her on the forehead. "No goddamn terrorists are going to change our way of life, I'll guarantee you that." He had forgotten about his determination to leave Washington as he turned, grabbed his briefcase off the hood of the car, and started walking toward the terminal. He could hear Donna sobbing. *Jeez, we've got to stay positive.* He could picture her wiping her eyes and watching him. *We can't get paranoid. This fuckin' evil can't shut our country down.*

The security guard held up his hand with his palm almost in Troy's face and motioned for Troy to put his briefcase on the small table outside the terminal door.

If we aren't careful, this could change our way of life forever. Troy was boiling inside. *We allowed too many fundamental changes during the past thirty years.* The security guard was looking through the briefcase. *Our leaders got too involved and wrapped up outside the country, and our courts went nuts in the name of individual freedoms.* He recalled his discussion with Harry, who he'd finally been able to contact yesterday. *Thank God Harry and his family are okay.* The guard was looking at him. *Jeez man, why're you looking at me like that?* The guard pushed the briefcase toward Troy and waved his arm as if to say, "Get out of here."

As he entered the terminal, he thought, *This is a dream, a nightmare!* He passed through two more security checks on his way to the departure lounge. The lounge was almost empty. He selected a seat near the departure gate, put his briefcase on the floor, and looked up into the expressionless eyes of the armed guard positioned by the gate.

The American Airlines Boeing 767 was only twenty per cent full. It seemed empty. Troy tried to anticipate the issues he would face on the Hill. *We need to take immediate action, not just to help New York recover but to fix our security. Jeez, how did we let it happen?* His mind flashed through terrorist-centred rumours that had been circulating on the Hill for months. *No one anticipated or speculated anything like this, at least not to my knowledge.*

The flight attendant took his order for a cup of coffee and a glass of orange juice. Troy's focus shifted to international issues as she walked away. *The president's talking about an international coalition to apprehend and bring the terrorists to justice. We don't even know who did it!* Suddenly his mind filled with rage. *It was the evilest act against our country since Pearl Harbor. Those responsible must pay.* His muscles tightened. *They will pay dearly.* He closed his eyes and breathed deeply. *Getting an effective coalition could be impossible. Shit, for the past six or seven months the White House has been telling most of the world to go screw itself.*

The flight attendant put coffee and orange juice on his tray. As he swigged the orange juice down in one gulp, another thought hit him. *If the Arabs join a coalition with us, they'll insist we address the terror in Palestine.* More complications came to mind as he sipped his coffee. A chill went up his back, down his arms, into his fingers. He put his cup back on the tray and unconsciously began to twirl the cup in a circle. *The CIA says bin Laden's behind the attacks. Al-Qaeda's main camps are in Afghanistan.* He shook his head and bit his lower lip. *Shit, we helped set up that whole Taliban operation when they were fighting the Russians. Damn it. Too many international ventures end up backfiring on us.*

Troy sipped coffee as the flight attendant set the breakfast plate on his tray, then handed her the cup for a refill. As she left, he wondered who would join a coalition. *Canada's a given, and Japan. The Middle East nations?* He shook his head. *They're all Muslim.* His stomach gurgled. He grabbed the fork, jabbed it into a green grape, and put it in his mouth as the attendant put the filled coffee cup back on his tray. *They provide half of our oil imports. The stupidity of it all!* He shifted in his seat, his knees banged the tray support, and coffee slopped over the edge of the cup. *Those nations hate us, mostly because of our policies in Israel.* He tried to focus on obvious friends. *Maybe Saudi Arabia, Qatar, and the Arab Emirates would join a coalition, but first we'll need to prove who's responsible for the attack. King Abdullah condemned the attack, but he'll want the question of Palestinian sovereignty resolved. They all will. And Iraq. Shit.* He forced a silent laugh. *We've been bombing them continually since 1993. Maybe Saddam's behind all this!*

Troy bit into another grape. His stomach reacted and he swallowed quickly to prevent bile from getting to his mouth.

In the days that followed, Washington considered the nine-eleven attacks an act of war against the United States. The CIA and other U.S. security agencies quickly established that Osama bin Laden and his al Qaeda terrorist network were behind the attacks, and that bin Laden was living in Afghanistan. President Bush demanded that Afghanistan's Taliban leadership hand bin Laden over to the United

States and expel al Qaeda from that country, but the Taliban refused to do so without clear and undisputable evidence of bin Laden's involvement in the attack.

On October 7, 2001, the United States and Britain launched attacks, code named Operation Enduring Freedom, against Afghanistan and its Taliban leadership. Other NATO nations provided support, the Taliban was quickly driven from political power, and NATO military bases were built near major cities as most of the al Qaeda and Taliban forces escaped to remote mountainous regions and into neighbouring Pakistan. In December, Hamid Karzai was selected to head the new Afghan administration.

Within a year, the White House's focus was back to Iraq and Saddam Hussein.

CHAPTER 5

RETIREMENT & MORE CONCERNS

A few years later

It was a warm mid-week evening in August 2006. Troy and Donna had been retired from Washington for over a year. They were both sixty-two. Although federal politics never seemed to be far from their minds, their primary attention was centred on their children's families. Leslie's family lived in Temecula, an easy twenty-minute drive from her parents' home in San Diego. Tim's construction company was successful and their daughter and younger son were both in grade school. Jeff and Colleen's son and younger daughter were still in pre-school. Jeff had plans to leave Scripps and start up his own consulting business, specializing in high-tech computer services required by the medical industry. Their Del Mar home was also within easy driving distance.

Troy was tending steaks on the barbeque in the shaded area near the back of the house. Most of the rest of the yard was drenched in late afternoon sun. Birds were chirping in the forest of trees beyond the back of the property and their schnauzer puppy, named Curly after their previous dog, sat inside the chain-link fence anxiously watching squirrels scramble through the trees. Troy's short-sleeve shirt and short pants exposed tanned and muscular arms and legs that, with the solid grey of his short hair and bushy eyebrows, gave him the appearance of a capable but aging athlete.

"How are those steaks doing?" Donna asked as she carried two sets of cutlery and napkins to the round glass-topped lawn table. She was well tanned and radiantly beautiful in a loose-fitting blouse, knee-length skirt, and sandals. "Can I top up your wine?" She set the stuff on the table and reached for the open bottle of red wine.

"Another two minutes for the steaks," Troy answered without looking up. "Is your part ready?"

"Potatoes and asparagus are ready. The steaks smell great. I'm hungry. I'll bring out the plates."

"Good." Troy flipped the steaks and added a final shot of barbeque sauce while Donna topped up their wine.

Minutes later, Donna was back at Troy's side with plates of baked potatoes and asparagus. Troy put the steaks on the plates and turned the barbeque off. Donna was seated, and Curly was under the table with her nose in the air, when Troy sat down.

"Are you going to say grace?" Donna asked.

"Yah, I guess." Troy gave a short blessing.

"Cheers." Donna held out her wine glass.

"Cheers, dear." It seemed absentminded.

As their glasses clicked, Donna asked, "What's bothering you, honey?"

He smiled and looked into her eyes. "You can read me like a book, can't you?" He sipped his wine. "Frankly, I'm getting bored with this retired life."

"What do you mean?" She was honestly surprised. "You never stop. You're going all the time; to see the kids and their families, the work you do around the yard and the house." Her mind was loaded with examples. "Exercising every day, teaching Curly new tricks, our golf games and walks along the ocean, your snips group, all the other stuff. Honey, how can you be bored?"

Troy had started eating and Donna cut into her steak. Curly was watching closely, hoping something would drop to the ground. Tory tried recalling some of the other things that had taken his attention since retirement. *That retirement party in Washington was quite the send-off! The only time I've thought about federal affairs since then is when our snips group gets off the course and the guys want me to explain why the hell George W. keeps Cheney and Rumsfeld around. Somehow, they manage to laugh when I tell them I'm wondering the same thing.* They were well into their meal before Troy was ready to answer Donna's question. He sipped his wine, then turned to look into her eyes. She returned his look.

"You know, I love doing all those things, but it's just not me. I can't pretend to enjoy myself while I watch our country slipping in directions that really concern me."

"I know you're concerned, but—" She wasn't sure what to say.

Troy cleaned all but a last piece of steak from his plate. "I'm sick and tired of our news networks, both the papers and television. They're continuously questioning and second-guessing the leaders we elect, pretending they're speaking for the people of this nation." He put his knife and fork on the plate and looked into her eyes. "The whole direction of our country has changed so damn much over the past four decades. It's out of the hands of Washington. The White House and Congress give so much attention to global issues, they have no time to deal effectively with our domestic economy."

He grabbed the last bite of meat and flipped it to the ground in front of Curly.

Donna did the same as Troy emptied the wine bottle into their glasses.

"Our economy's being run to ground by bankers and Wall Street," Troy continued. "Everyone seems to be going deeper and deeper in debt. Our major corporations are focused on maximizing quarterly profits instead of providing good long-term employment and service to America and Americans." He sipped the wine and looked at her over the edge of the glass. "We're in trouble." He put his glass on the table. "And our churches are just as much to blame as Washington."

"What? What have they got to do with it?"

"I know. That statement sounds strange, but it's true. One of the guys in the foursome yesterday was ranting that our Christian base has totally eroded. You know, things like removing the Lord's Prayer from public places, replacing Merry Christmas with Happy Holidays, the gay rights stuff, the priests we can't trust; all that stuff. He went on and on, trying to describe his theory that Christians made a big mistake back in the '60s and '70s when they didn't embrace evolution as a newly discovered part of God's plan. He got into some detail I couldn't argue with." Troy took a deep breath. "And he said church leaders should have held firm years ago, should have told the liberal whiners they could leave America if they didn't like living in our Christian nation." He stood and started to gather dishes. "The more I thought about it, the more I agreed with him, despite what the First Amendment says. In fact, I told him the only times I could remember Christian lobbyists coming to see me when I was in Washington was when they were after money for some evangelical thing or, and I really surprised myself saying this, supporting some Zionist cause." He started walking to the house with his hands full.

Donna stood and cleared the rest of the dishes from the table. "You're right, honey," she yelled as Troy stood holding the door open. "Things have changed a lot since we were married." Her hands were full as she walked toward the house. "I'm so glad you left Washington when you did." She stopped and looked up into his eyes. "I love you, Mr. Rogers."

Two years later
September 2008.

Few American families were immune from the financial crisis that hit the United States in September when, on the sixteenth of the month, the nation's largest insurance company begged the Federal Reserve Board for a $40-billion loan to cover the losses it had suffered as a result of a widespread, mismanaged, and fraudulent house of cards created by the nation's banking and financial industries. It was the tip of a financial iceberg that smashed into America's economy and created the largest and longest financial crisis in the history of the Western world.

Troy was furious with the way Washington politicians decided to handle the crisis. "Careless and high-risk policies invented by financial institutions and many other major corporations are destroying our economy," became his favourite one-liner explanation for what had happened. Before a week was out, he called Harry to get his assessment of the situation.

"Everyone's puzzled," Harry agreed during their long telephone discussion. "But frankly, I saw this coming years ago. Our financial networks—the banks, insurance companies, and all the Wall Street brokerage houses—led the charge. They were allowed to consolidate ownerships in all that financial power. It's a greedy bunch, and consolidating that greed would turn any economy on its head." He grunted in disgust. "The worse thing Washington could have done is leave those responsible for the whole mess in charge of managing a solution, and that's what they did! They let them off the hook and handed over trillions more in public debt so those crooks can continue to play their greedy schemes. How dumb is that?!" He cleared his throat. "Makes no sense to me. Seems everyone in authority is afraid to admit what's been happening over the past couple of decades. There isn't an easy solution, Troy. Everyone seems afraid to deal with the tough questions except—" He stopped.

"Except who?"

"Oh, this guy I know who owns one of the smaller communication networks operating out of midtown Manhattan." He laughed. "The only guy I know who really tells it the way it is."

"Is he Jewish? Why doesn't he tell all of us the real truth?" The questions came out of nowhere and Troy could not believe how he'd phrased his thoughts.

There was an awkward silence before Harry reacted. "Troy, you're making me feel like when I was in your congressional office several years ago, when you accused all Jews of reacting as one for Israel! Then, and now, I say fuck you, buddy." He coughed. "You've got to learn not to look at all of us as part of a single Zionist conspiracy!"

Troy half expected to hear the line go dead, but it didn't.

"I didn't mean it that way, Harry. Surely, you know that. I only—"

"I know, Troy. But it's a very touchy thing for me and many others. You've got to watch out how you say things."

"Sorry. But really, sometime I'd like to hear what that newspaper friend of yours considers to be the honest truth."

"Don't hold your breath. I've got to go." Harry laughed. "In the meantime, hold whatever money you've still got really close to your chest."

"I will, Harry. Keep well." He hung up.

Early Fall 2009

The subject of the faltering and mismanaged economy was to remain a major topic of discussion in America and most of the Western world for years to come.

Donna and Troy wandered together hand-in-hand on a relatively secluded beach in La Jolla one warm, sunny mid-week afternoon. They were both wearing broad-peaked hats and sunglasses as protection against the bright sun, and were focused on counting the number of sails they could see in the peaceful Pacific water to the west.

"I get forty," Donna said.

"I'm not that high yet; and I'm tired of counting." Troy kicked the sand with his right foot. "This sand is still nice and warm."

"Hopefully we've got another month of it before things start to get colder."

They walked in silence for a few minutes, both wondering much the same thing. Donna finally broke the silence. "I'm puzzled. I keep reading that the major banks are recovering and are again paying huge bonuses to their executives. That can't be, can it? Not while everyone else is still suffering so much. What am I missing?"

Troy shrugged. "You're not missing anything, honey. Our politicians are simply afraid to challenge those Shylocks."

"Maybe you should have stayed in Washington."

He laughed. "You don't mean that!"

"Will things ever change?"

Troy kicked the sand again and shook his head. "I doubt it. Even though some might feel there have been a few key changes since Obama took over the White House last January." Barak Obama was America's first African-American president. "It's hard to imagine much really changing. Washington is so stagnant and loaded with partisanship. I think the international bankers and our media networks are setting the whole agenda." He chuckled. "How would you like to be Obama right now?"

Donna shook her head. "I'd gladly pass on that." She tilted the peak of her hat back with her right hand and looked up at Troy. There was a smile on her face. She squeezed his hand tight. "I'm very happy with our life just the way it is."

A few days later, Troy and Donna visited Jeff and his family for Sunday dinner at their home in Del Mar. It was mid-afternoon, the children were on the front street rollerblading with neighbourhood friends and Donna was helping Colleen in the kitchen. Troy and Jeff were relaxed on chairs in the sunny section of the large patio at the back of the house. They were both wearing light jackets and long pants as protection against a cool westerly breeze. Two cans of Bud Lite and a bowl of mixed nuts sat on the shaded section created by the umbrella in the centre of the large, round patio table. Far in the distance to the south, they could see the Coastal Highway cutting through the stretch of pine trees along the ridge north of the Torrey Pines Golf Club.

Jeff was forty and his computer services consulting company was doing well. Other than the thick, long, wavy well-groomed dark-brown hair that covered a portion of his ears and the back of his neck, he seemed the image of his father at the same age. Troy was starting to show his years; his short hair was totally grey, there were a few facial wrinkles, the sparkle was gone from eyes dimmed by the hint of mild cataracts, and there was an almost unnoticeable slump in his powerful shoulders.

Troy lifted his beer and tapped Jeff's can. "Cheers, son. It's good to see the family so well."

"Thanks, Dad. You and Mom are looking good. It's been a few weeks."

"Where does time go?"

Jeff grinned. "In this house, time flies trying to keep up with the kids."

"I bet. They both look good and seem really happy. Good for you and Colleen. How old are they now?" He thought for a second before answering his own question. "Caleb's five, Katie three, right?"

"Yep, and they're both a handful!"

"When you and Leslie were that age, I think we had just moved to Edmonton. Those were good days."

For a while they recalled the names of Edmonton neighbours and friends. Jeff finished his beer, stood and started toward the house. "I'll get us another one." Troy closed his eyes and tried to gather warmth from the sinking sun.

When Jeff returned and settled back into his chair he asked, "How would you like to be in Obama's shoes, Dad?"

Troy laughed. "Thanks for the beer." He finished off the first can. "I wouldn't." He cracked the tab of the new can.

"He's facing so many critical issues. Where will he start?"

Troy nodded as a few of the issues came to mind. "We're mired in military engagements in Iraq and Afghanistan. Osama bin Laden is still at large. There's growing instability in several Islamic nations. Problems in Israel and Palestine continue to fester. The EU and NATO keep pushing further into old Soviet territories, and I think that's asking for trouble. And during—"

"What's that EU and NATO stuff about?" Jeff interrupted. "Sometimes I wonder if they're trying to create another war."

"I know what you mean. Wonder that myself sometimes. I had an interesting talk with Jacob's dad not long ago." Troy swigged his beer. "He's angry and bothered. Thinks our misdirected economy and the EU stuff is all orchestrated by powerful European networks."

"Like the International Monetary Fund? Or World Bank? Or European Central Bank?"

"Includes those for sure."

Jeff laughed. "There's more?"

"Who knows?" Troy turned and looked west. "Boy, when that sun starts to sink—"

"It cools off pretty quickly. You okay?"

"For now." He got back on topic. "Harry says a lot of powerful European bankers fled to Switzerland during the Nazi regime because it was a neutral country. Says that's where international monetary power now rests." He paused. "He's become concerned that—"

"Jeff!" Colleen called through the screened window in the kitchen. "Please get the kids in to wash up for dinner. We'll be eating in fifteen minutes."

Jeff stood and finished his beer. "I'll get the kids, Dad. Finish your beer, and let's not talk politics during dinner."

Six years later
Late January 2015; San Diego

Troy and Donna were in the den of their San Diego home watching the 5:00 p.m. TST NEWS. Both were seventy years old. Troy reached for the remote.

"A couple of days ago, House Speaker Boehner invited Israeli Prime Minister Netanyahu to address Congress," TST NEWS anchor Carol Fulton said. "He made the invite without consulting President Obama or the White House."

Troy removed his finger from the off button and focused on Ms. Fulton's report. "Our sources indicate the meeting was the brainchild of AIPAC, which is one of the lobby organizations that hopes to accumulate the sixty-seven congressional votes needed to overturn any veto President Obama might decide to use against a congressional effort to increase existing sanctions against Iran. Other sources indicate this may simply be a move by Netanyahu to enhance his chances for re-election in Israel's upcoming election and—"

Troy hit the off button and slammed the remote down on the arm of his chair. "This has the same rotten stench as when Shamir and his lobbyists corralled all those votes against President Bush senior's re-election hopes in the early nineties. It's disgusting!" He pounded the arms of the chair in frustration. "I remember when Netanyahu lied to us about Iraq having nuclear and chemical weapons after nine-eleven. I'll never forgive myself for agreeing to send our troops on that mission, into harm's way. I'll never forget that! We need to—"

"I can't believe it either," Donna interrupted as she stood and stretched. "Have you spoken with Harry Grumner lately? He always gives you a pretty good perspective on those things."

"We talked a couple of weeks ago. I doubt if he had any idea about this new initiative."

"Let's go to bed."

Troy stood and walked behind Donna to the bedroom. As they settled into bed twenty minutes later, Donna asked, "Who do you think will win the White House in 2016? Who will the Republicans nominate as their candidate?"

Troy closed his eyes and took a deep breath. "Partisanship has ruined our federal government," he said without answering the question. "I expect it won't really matters who gets in." He was almost asleep. "Sleep well, dear."

CHAPTER 6

ANY SOLUTION?

Early Fall, 2016; San Diego

The 2016 U.S. presidential election was a month away. Opinion polls indicated a huge majority of Americans wanted to see major changes in Washington and that partisanship feelings between Democrats and Republicans were at an all-time high.

It was a warm and sunny mid-afternoon in San Diego. Troy and Donna were both seventy-two years old and in excellent health. He was in a deep sleep on the patio couch when the phone rang in the house. Thirty seconds later, Donna tapped him on the shoulder.

"Wake up, dear. This is for you. A surprise."

It took Troy a few seconds to come out of his deep sleep. He shifted to a sitting position, rubbed his eyes and smiled at Donna as she handed him the telephone. "Hello?" He had no idea who would be calling.

"Hi, Troy. It's Harry. How are—?"

"Harry!" Troy was suddenly wide awake. "How are you? What's the occasion?"

"I'll be in your area next week. We're spending a week in Rancho Mirage, with Jacob and his fiancé at her parents' home there. I'd like to drive over to San Diego and see you."

"It's a nothing week for me, Harry. Any time you say. Rebecca will be with you?"

"No, she'll stay in the desert. I'd like to have a private discussion with you."

"Sure, okay. Jacob can give you directions to the house." They talked for a while longer and agreed to meet the next Wednesday.

Harry arrived at Troy's house six days later. It was about noon and there was still a light fog in the air. Troy half-ran to the front door when the bell rang, their eyes met, and they both had wide grins on their faces.

"Harry!" Troy grabbed his friend's outstretched hand. "Good to see you. You look great! How was your drive?"

"The drive was easy. I'm glad to get a break from the desert heat. You look pretty damn good yourself."

They exchanged pleasantries and settled into two leather chairs facing each other across a small coffee table in the den. Donna had set the table with coffee and plates of small one-bite sandwiches and cookies before going to visit their daughter in Temecula.

Troy leaned forward, grabbed the thermos, filled the mugs, and pointed to the plates. "These plates—your mom and dad gave them to us as a wedding gift. We use them whenever we have guests over."

Harry smiled. "That's really nice to know."

Troy looked into Harry's dark eyes. "What's on your mind?"

"Before we get to that, I want to thank your family for making Jacob feel so welcome in your home. He really thinks a lot of you."

"We think he's a good guy, Harry. A chip off the old block."

They spent the next twenty minutes eating most of the sandwiches and cookies and talking about family before there was an awkward silence.

Harry decided to tell a story. "Yesterday, Rebecca came home from a fundraiser with an interesting story from one of the ladies," he said straight-faced. "A twenty-five-year-old Jewish girl told her mother that she had missed her period for two months. Very worried, the mother went to the local pharmacy, bought a pregnancy test kit, and the test confirmed her daughter was pregnant. Shouting and crying, the mother demanded, 'Who was the foolish devil that did this to you?' Without answering her mother, the girl picked up the phone and made a call. Half an hour later, a Bentley stopped in front of their home and a distinguished middle-aged man got out and entered the house. He sat on the lounge with the girl's father and mother and told them, 'I can't marry her because of my personal family situation, but I'll take charge. I'll pay all costs and provide for your daughter for the rest of her life. Additionally, if a girl is born, I will bequeath two retail furniture stores, a deli, a chateau in France, and a one-million-pound bank account. If a boy is born, my legacy will be a chain of jewellery stores and a 25-million-pound bank account. However, if there is a miscarriage, I'm not sure what to do. What would you suggest?' There was total silence. Finally, the mother turned, placed a hand firmly on the man's shoulder and said, 'You try again.'"

They both laughed. "I need to tell Donna that one," Troy said.

"Thought you'd like it." Harry leaned forward, grabbed his coffee mug in his left hand, took a sip, put it back on the table and looked into Troy's eyes. "Everyone in New York thinks the upcoming election will be brutal. Lots of hidden stuff likely to surface. I'm afraid—" he paused and his next word seemed unconnected. "Balkanization."

"Pardon. Balkanization?"

Harry cleared his throat. "So many things have been mismanaged. There's an avalanche of problems and challenges."

Troy nodded and half-chuckled. "Don't I know! When I was in Washington we seemed helpless to—"

"I know, I know. By the time you left there the bankers were building their wide-ranging networks into a debt-ridden paper pyramid. Since then they've taken us into deeper waters while partisanship cripples Congress."

Troy grunted in disgust. "Glad I got out of there when I did. Seems like just yesterday, but it's been over a dozen years!" He shook his head in disbelief. "I thought we should have let the bankers and their equity owners pay for all the consequences of their schemes when things collapsed in 2008."

"Me too," Harry agreed. "But the FED and IMF sold the White House and Congress on that too-big-to-fail bullshit."

Another disgusted grunt. "And the big-money boys probably used most of that bailout money and their quantitative easing scheme to consolidate their ownerships in corporations here and around the world."

"Yeah." Harry took a deep breath. "We screwed up. America's leaders screwed up!" He rubbed his forehead in frustration. "Americans are angry, and they should be! We've not yet realized the full magnitude of it all." He paused. "So many of our major corporations have relocated outside the country to escape taxes. Young professionals can't find jobs; they're about to realize they'll be the only ones left to eventually clean up the whole mess. We've got huge gaps between our rich and poor, high unemployment, homelessness, university graduates and young homeowners with crippling debt obligations. Religious institutions are giving conflicting moral messages." He coughed to clear his throat, then forced a chuckle. "Hell, Troy, I wouldn't be surprised if we suddenly discover that tens of thousands of tons of our gold reserves have somehow disappeared from Fort Knox! It's mindboggling how we ever allowed ourselves to get to this point!" Harry cleared his throat again. "History gives a clear tell of who will eventually be blamed when the whole thing finally hits a wall."

Troy said nothing.

Harry swallowed hard, grabbed the mug and finished his coffee. "Troy, you're a Christian." He paused. "You probably know little about the Jewish religion." Troy nodded. "We have a long history," Harry continued, "and I've been doing a lot of reading and thinking about that over the past couple of years."

Troy shrugged. "I admit, even after all my Bible reading and time in Washington, I don't really understand the fundamental difference between Christians and Jews in America. Except," he forced a laugh, "the Jews have all the money, control the lobbyists in Washington, and dictate what we hear on our major television newscasts." He looked into Harry's eyes. "What are the differences anyway?"

Harry smiled. "I'm probably too simplistic."

"Tell me."

Harry took a while to answer. "Simplistically, I understand Christian teachings, and Islamic teachings too, focus on the importance of preparing souls and spirits for life after death. In contrast, our Jewish religion focuses on living today, right now, in this life;

we believe this is where our souls and spirits experience life to the fullest. That's about it, in real simple terms."

"I've never heard it expressed in that way." Troy thought for a moment. "So, Jews control money and markets and the media because—"

Harry's laugh drowned him out. "No, come on now!" He paused. "But, in order to do our best here on earth, those things are sure among the most powerful means to do it." He paused. "In that regard, I think an awful lot of powerful Christians have become Judaists as far as their business practices are concerned!" There was a short silence. "Anyway, that's my simplistic opinion."

"So," Troy paused, "all the focus on money, markets, big estates, all that stuff: the rationale is that those accomplishments please God right here on earth? Do love and caring have any place in—?"

Harry nodded. "You know, Troy, for most Jews those things are always there. Money, laws, and so on would get us nowhere in our effort to please God without love for fellow Jews and other friends. But our focus is on this life, not some afterlife promise."

Troy felt stuck for something to say and several seconds passed. "So, what's all that got to do with balkanization?"

Harry took his time. "If our economy crashes and Americans become much angrier than they already are, they'll need to take their anger out on something, someone. History suggests that focus is bound to rest on those who have run our economy into the ground and have us around the neck with debt and other financial obligations." He paused to grab his mug. It was empty but he kept both hands around it. "A disproportionate number of Jews are at the strategic and operational hearts of banking, finance, and money market operations in America and throughout the Western world.

That's just how it is. And they'll be easy to single out and blame, just like always. It happened many times in the past; the last in Germany about the time you and I were born. Why not America's turn early in this century?" He paused for a deep breath. "Except, thanks to our gun laws and the massive accumulation of arms throughout our country, it's bound to be different. Would probably result in more than one civil war and end in some form of balkanization."

Troy felt like the wind had been knocked out of him. *It couldn't happen!* "What can be done about it, Harry?"

"I've asked myself the same question. Unfortunately, the world banking network is unbreakable. With the IMF, ECB, FED, all the banks and other financial institutions. It's like a whole separate world empire that's holding the puppet strings of the economies of all Western nations."

There was a long and uncomfortable silence. Troy tried to calm himself by pouring more coffee, but neither picked up his mug. He extended the plate of cookies to Harry, who just shook his head. Finally, Troy asked, "How about a scotch?"

Harry's lips were tight together but his eyes opened wide and he nodded. Nothing was said while Troy got the scotch bottle and glasses from a cabinet across the room and poured their drinks. He handed Harry's drink to him and picked up his own. They clicked their glasses as friends will do. Each had taken a few sips before Troy finally broke the silence.

"Balkanization can't be allowed to play out, Harry."

"I agree, but honestly, I don't see how it can be stopped at this point. That's why I wanted to speak with you."

Troy's mind was racing and he absentmindedly topped up their glasses. "Maybe with the election coming up, it's a good time."

"What's on your mind?"

Troy shrugged. "Nothing." He sipped the scotch, then held the glass at arm's length and focused on the soothing colour. When he turned back to Harry there was contentment in his eyes. "But I know as well as I'm sitting here that you and I have got some thinking to do."

"I agree," Harry raised his glass. "A toast to another challenge together."

Troy raised his glass. "To another challenge."

A few months later
Mid-January 2017

It was late afternoon in mid-week. Troy and his son Jeff had just completed a round of golf at the club and were sitting at a patio table with two mugs of beer, tall glasses of water, and a large plate of cheese-laden nachos. Far in the west, the sea was quiet, the sun was almost over the horizon, and the sky was multiple peaceful shades of red and purple.

"What a life!" Troy chuckled. "Not many guys in this world are as lucky as me. Thanks for taking the day off for this, Jeff."

"Wouldn't have missed it for the world, Dad. It was fun. We both hit some good ones. Your knees held out okay, didn't they?"

"No problem. I'm lucky." Troy laughed as he grabbed a few nachos from the plate. "And I only lost one of the balls the kids gave me for Christmas."

Jeff smiled as he reached for nachos. Troy grabbed his mug. There was a long silence.

"Christmas at the house was really fun. You and Mom have always put on a wonderful dinner, but I'm glad she agreed to let

Colleen and Leslie take turns at our houses from now on. It's just too much for you guys."

"We've always loved doing it, but you're right. Time for a change."

There was another long silence as they dove into the nachos and ordered coffee. "Talk about change: the whole world seems to be speculating about changes here in the next few weeks."

"Trump's not even waiting." Jeff laughed. "He tweets every morning about what should be happening."

"Thank goodness he'll stop that tweeting nonsense once he gets into the White House," Troy sighed. "I don't even know what tweeting is."

"Young Americans are on their computers and cellphones all day, Dad. They read the tweets and everything else. What's really scary is that most of them believe everything they read. I'm like you; I hope Trump's tweets stop as soon as he gets into the White House, but I wouldn't bet on it!" Jeff suddenly remembered something he'd intended to mention earlier. "I had lunch with Jacob Grumner last week."

"How's Jacob doing?"

"Good, but he doesn't like Trump. Thinks he might know what needs to be done to get the country back on track, but isn't really someone with a presidential presence."

Troy thought of the discussion he had with Harry months earlier. "I'm sure Jacob and his father think alike. We'll all just have to wait and see what unfolds." He looked at his watch. "We'd better get out of here or we'll be late for dinner."

Three months later
Early April 2017; New York City

Troy and Donna flew to New York City for the funeral of a retired senator who had been especially close to them during their days in Washington. They decided to stay at a Marriott Hotel on Times Square and spend a few extra days experiencing some of the Big Apple's adventures. The second evening they took the Grumners to dinner at the revolving restaurant in the hotel.

"Let's not talk politics," Troy whispered to Harry as the ladies settled into their seats.

"I heard that!" Rebecca laughed. "And you'd better not, if you fellows know what's good for you!"

It was a perfect start to a charming evening that was filled with fine food, countless family stories, and lots of laughs. Three hours later, they all stood together outside the hotel waiting for a taxi to take the Grumners home.

"You're going to the theatre tomorrow night," Harry said to Troy. "Think you've got time for a beer at my favourite midtown bar about 1:00?"

Troy looked at Donna. "Do it," she said. "I want to shop."

Early the next afternoon, Troy and Harry were sitting on tall chairs at a small round table in a quiet corner of the bar, their jackets over the backs of the chairs. Two mugs of beer and a bowl of mixed nuts sat on the table. It didn't take long for them to start discussing President Trump's cabinet appointments and how a Republican-controlled Congress could be expected to expedite approval of anything Trump wanted.

"The only fly in the ointment is the rumour that Russia interfered in the election," Harry said. "The media won't let it—"

"The media's worse than when I was in Washington!" Troy interrupted. "Most of them can't get over Trump defeating Hillary. Some even seem to want Obama back in the White House!" He grabbed his mug. "Trump's got to clean out the swamp of lobbyists in both Congress and our major media outlets before Washington can operate properly again." He gulped down a mouthful of beer. "The media focus on the Russian thing—" He laughed. "How many years have our intelligence networks been interfering in elections around the world!?" He thought of the time he and Harry met in his office on the hill about thirty years ago. "And I don't recall the media ever once complaining about Israel's meddling in our politics over the past half-century!"

"I agree." Harry put his mug on the table and grabbed a few nuts. "It reminds me of our discussion at your place in San Diego last fall." He paused. "I've followed up a bit on what we discussed with an old acquaintance. I might have mentioned him to you before; Adam Goldsilva. He used to be a top antitrust lawyer, then became sole owner and manager of a small and provocative media network here in New York a few years ago. He's considered a real renegade by most New Yorkers, but he's opened my eyes with some of his historical knowledge and opinions."

He took a swig, cleared his throat, and looked across at Troy. "Adam believes that the economy of any pure democracy will eventually be completely taken over by those controlling that nation's money supply, unless there are strong and strictly applied antitrust regulations. He believes that, without those regulations being very carefully constructed, elected officials really have no effective

79

influence or control over the power of money. After the discussions you and I had, and listening to Adam, I'm convinced that, combined with the make-up of our Central Bank and our toothless gun control laws, disregard of our old antitrust regulations is destroying America. Adam thinks the 2016 election might be the last peaceful election our country will ever see."

"You're kidding!" Troy reached for his mug.

"No, I'm not. Adam says the only hope for our economy is to break up all the centralized controls and ownerships that have developed in our key industries. It's hard to name an industry where it hasn't happened. We habitually point at banking, brokerage, oil, and railways; but there are so many others. Adam says breaking up that centralized control will result in more jobs, more competition, and better accountability. He thinks we'd maybe need new tariff and border control regulations to protect our markets from cheaper imports, but that's better than just giving everything over to the world money boys." Harry chuckled. "Adam also says we need to get back on the gold standard." His voice had become so quiet, Troy was leaning across the table with both hands cupped over his ears. "According to him, our leaders don't put enough focus on learning from others, so our democracy just repeats the same old mistakes. He says the seeds of many of our problems were scattered in 1917—exactly a hundred years ago."

"What do you mean?" Troy leaned back in his chair.

"He's convinced three world events in 1917 set the whole stage for the future direction of our country." Harry smiled. "Bet you a hundred bucks you can't name them."

Troy grabbed some nuts and sipped his beer. *World War One, but what else?* He tried to think. *Hmm, 1917? I can't think; my mind's too filled with current issues.* He put his mug on the table, looked across at Harry, and shrugged. "You win. I got World War I, but what else happened?"

Harry smiled. "World War I started in 1914, but you're close. The United States entered that war in 1917. It was also the year the Russian Revolution started. And it was the year the British government signed the Balfour Declaration and agreed to support the Zionist initiative to establish a homeland for the Jewish people in Palestine." He shrugged. "Adam says, and I think I agree with him, those were the initial seeds for our problems today."

They munched on nuts, sipped beer, and were lost in their own private thoughts for several silent moments.

"What about right now, in 2017?" Troy finally asked.

Harry smiled. "I can picture Adam reacting to the question." He chuckled. "He'd be chewing on the stump of a fat cigar that always sticks out of the left corner of his mouth and smoke would fill the air. I expect he'd still make some reference to history. He always does. Would probably go back to the Second World War. I know he believes Britain's decline after winning that war was a major disaster for us here in America."

"How's that?" Troy reacted.

Harry scratched his head, trying to recall things Goldsilva had mentioned to him in the past. "I expect he'd point out that, after that war, there were only three major powers left. Us, the Brits, and the Soviets. We all had to focus on rebuilding domestic economies that had suffered as a result of the war. The Brits had the biggest challenge by far." He paused. "And they were also still responsible for managing and keeping peace in their Palestinian Mandate, which really became a problem. They eventually gave up that mandate, leaving the responsibility to the United Nations. If that hadn't happened, if Britain had been strong enough to force a peaceful and lasting development of Israel and Palestine," he paused, "I expect everything would have come out okay. But, because the British withdrew and the UN couldn't coup with the challenge, we Americans got caught in the trap." He grabbed his mug and took a few sips.

"I think I understand," Troy offered. "If the British had been able to maintain control in Palestine, our only interest in the Middle East would have been the Arab oilfields, and…"

"Right," Harry placed his mug on the table and grabbed a few nuts. "But when war-ravaged Jews kept flocking into Israel after the British left, we quickly got caught between our need for oil and demands for support of Israel. Washington's been torn apart ever since."

"It sure screwed up our whole energy situation."

"For sure. I remember that story; the one you told me back in the late eighties, when we were in your office at the Capitol." New thoughts were racing into Harry's mind. "When I told Adam that story, about the oil weapon and America's Achilles' heel, he immediately got talking about how different our Constitution might have been if our Founding Fathers had any idea that our leaders in Washington would end up spending so much time and budget allocations on Middle East issues, and all the other serious considerations so far from our borders."

"What do you mean?"

Harry laughed. "Among all the other things Adam is, he's an expert on our Constitution." He paused. They both munched on some nuts and had a couple of swigs of beer. Finally: "Adam says our Constitution was fundamentally developed to hold our lands, our states, the American people; all together as an effective republic. The innovative Constitutional format developed by the Founding Fathers, with our unique election processes and the checks-and-balances between the two legislatures, executive, and judicial branches; that was all designed with a very mature understanding of the differing passions of the states and the representatives they would elect to the federal government. I expect there was never any anticipation of having to police, finance, and administer lands and people halfway across the world!"

"I get it." Troy wiggled in his chair and waived at the barmaid to bring them another mug of beer.

They sat in silence, thinking about what had been said and letting it all sink in.

Harry's thoughts eventually returned to the economic issues facing Washington. He finished his beer, wondering how to best express what was on his mind. Finally, in a quiet voice: "Adam is quite a critic of Washington's handling of our economy. I expect, as is his habit, he'd even trace that issue historically." He paused, hoping Troy was with him. "He'd probably point out that, although European Christians of various denominations opened America's economy, it was also heavily colonized by Jews who were fleeing hundreds of years of European prejudice. I know he believes the whole framework of our economy has been heavily influenced by the descendants of those Jews, and thinks American capitalism today is now essentially a distillation of the Jewish spirit."

He sat back and took a deep breath as the barmaid arrived, placed full mugs on the table with a fresh bowl of nuts, took the empties, and left.

Troy broke the silence. "I'm not sure I'm with you, Harry."

Harry took a few swigs and gathered his thoughts for several seconds. "Christian entrepreneurs who came to America from all parts of Europe had an extraordinary vitality, a passionate joy in work, a humbling spiritual life, and a strong drive for social power and contribution. They thrived within a governing network that encouraged capital creation in a pretty fair, open, and competitive business environment. That was America's original capitalism. It focused on conservative financial management, creating jobs with long-term security, providing dedicated hands-on service to customers within a moral framework established by Christian beliefs, and supporting a progressive tax system that ensured the wealthy contributed the highest portions of their income to the state and national budgets of a growing U.S. economy." He paused for another swig. "Importantly, the term globalization was not really prominent in the lexicon of American business leaders until the late 1970s. But things have changed significantly over the years. Frankly, it's hard for me to imagine why Washington politicians just stood by and watched the destruction of that great model of capitalism."

"The lobbyists," Troy said. "You know my position on that. And technology has changed so—"

"At first we thought new technology would primarily be used to make most jobs easier," Harry said. "But instead, especially over the past few decades, it's been used to eliminate good jobs and cut costs for the sole benefit of wealthy shareholders. Antitrust regulations have been watered down, many totally forgotten, and business competition and jobs have been eliminated through consolidation of corporate ownerships. Risk-takers no longer pay for their own errors; the taxpayers do, largely because our government leaders are lobbied into thinking the large corporations are too big to fail."

Harry was on a roll and continued after a short breath. "Short-term profits, earnings growth rates, obscene executive bonuses, and international interests are now the focus in the boardrooms of our major corporations, rather than business ethics, customer service, financial stability, and employment security." A deep breath and another gulp of beer. "The biggest theft of all is that American billionaires and millionaires now pay millions to tax accountants in efforts to avoid paying taxes to the nation that made them wealthy, while our federal and state governments go deeper in debt each year! That's a complete insult to our country, our children, our teachers, police, firefighters, other first responders, military, and everyone else who—" Harry was so angry and out of breath he couldn't finish.

Troy put his mug to his mouth and swallowed a couple of times, wondering what to say.

"Adam's adamant that zero-sum philosophies have become the driving force behind what's now a destructive form of American and Western capitalism," Harry continued. "He's convinced that, without the governing constraints provided by sensible taxing and solid antitrust laws, capitalism becomes a highly predatory endeavour, with accumulation of money the fundamental objective, even of our elected officials."

"What about our military?"

Troy's question seemed out of context. Harry took a moment to react. "For some reason, U.S. and NATO investments in military initiatives continued aggressively after the end of the Cold War. I don't really understand why, other than maybe the lobby pressures associated with the globalization of international businesses, including the weapons manufacturers. Anyway, those initiatives continued to develop and operate at the cost of trillions of dollars per year to

Americans. And, as far as I'm concerned, it was mostly to maintain and protect the financial interests of banks, international corporations, and international entrepreneurs." He shrugged and forced a laugh. "It might be fun to see how they'd operate without our military at their backs."

Neither spoke for a couple of minutes as they alternated between the nuts and beer. Finally, Harry continued.

"Adam claims, and I agree with him, the American economy would be in much better shape today if, after the Cold War, we had focused primarily on developments within North America, this whole continent, and backed right away from any major government financial or military involvements in Asia and the Middle East. But we didn't, and so it's the Arab nations, Asians, and Israel that now have all the modern airports, freeways, rapid transit systems, new skyscrapers, infrastructure facilities, hi-tech medical research, and missile defence systems, while so many of our own continental defence and infrastructure facilities have become old and run-down."

"Any hope?" Troy asked with a chuckle.

Harry nodded. "Adam claims the only way out of the mess is to back out fast."

"Huh?"

"He says we need to return to our old model of capitalism. Focus on service, job creation, long-term security, antitrust regulations, conservative and responsible money management, a progressive tax system, so on. Focus within North America. Get rid of our zero-sum model of globalized capitalism."

Troy laughed. "What would the Devil say about that?"

Harry nodded, knowing the question required no response.

They finished their drinks in silence. Harry looked at his watch. "Can't believe we've been here over two hours. Wonder how many tweets Trump managed in that time?" He grinned, shuffled his chair back, and stood up.

Troy stood as the barmaid rushed over to give them the bill. Harry grabbed it, handed her three twenties, and followed Troy out the door.

The street seemed unusually quiet as Harry waved down a cab. They shook hands and he got into the back seat. "Talk to you soon," he yelled through the open window. "Have fun tonight, and a good trip back home tomorrow." The cab was moving.

"Keep well, Harry. Keep in touch," Troy shouted. He zipped up his jacket and headed back toward the hotel along breezy streets that were completely shaded by skyscrapers, picking up his paced to keep warm. *At least two police on each street,* he observed, remembering it was much the same when he walked to the bar earlier. Harry's comments kept racing through his mind, and he had an uneasy feeling in his gut as he turned a corner and was suddenly standing at the edge of Times Square.

People were rushing and brushing past him in all directions. *It's a packed house here.* He stood watching the kaleidoscope of world humanity. A five-storey neon sign was flashing on the side of his hotel about three blocks across the square. *Everyone's going in different directions.* He smiled to himself and a new thought suddenly struck. He started walking and watching eyes as he dodged through the clutter of people from dozens of nations, trying to guess who was from where, and how they might be feeling. They kept sweeping by and he started wondering: *Chinese Buddhist? Catholic? Jew? Hindu . . . East Indian? Greek? First Nations . . . Native American?*

Islamic Turk? Protestant . . . maybe Catholic? Syrian refugee? Arab or Persian? Atheist? His gaze lingered on two lovers: *French*, he thought, and then laughed to himself when they passed and he saw the maple leaf on the backward-facing ball cap: *Canadian.* Out of the corner of his eye, he saw a tramp bent over close to a building. *Something in his hands—jeez—a terrorist?* Suddenly, from nowhere, a muscular square-jawed guy and his female partner appeared on either side of the tramp, grabbed both of his arms and started patting him down. *Plain-clothed police or FBI.* As Troy continued walking, he could suddenly pick security personnel standing in pairs all over the place. *Some even dressed in clown outfits. They're operating in teams. Must be two security for every twenty tourists out here.* As he headed for the door of the hotel, he searched the outside of the building for security cameras. *I bet cameras are zeroed in on every square yard of Times Square.*

He was alone as he walked through the empty hotel lobby. *Outside suddenly felt like a police state*, he thought. A smile crossed his face as he pushed the up button for the elevator. *Sure felt safe and peaceful.* He watched the blinking lights as two of the three elevators descended.

THAT'S THE END OF THE FIRST STORY. WE'LL PICK UP WITH TROY AND DONNA ROGERS, and HARRY GRUMNER LATER.

Following are stories from elsewhere.

STORY 2

BRITAIN

CHAPTER 7

AN OLDER, BROADER PERSPECTIVE

Mid-September 2001; an estate on the fringe of London

James stood on the front porch of the large manor in southwest Britain and squinted into the sun-touched, mid-afternoon mist to watch the doctor's car disappear around the curve in the tree-lined drive. Tears streamed down his cheeks.

Doc gives m'Lord a few weeks at the most. James rubbed the tears away with a vein-filled hand, then looked at the bottle in his other hand. *Says these pills will keep him out of pain, so he can go on as normal, drinking his port and doing his writing.* James looked skyward. *What would I do without him?* He scratched his head, sending several strands of thick, wavy white hair across his forehead, then turned and grabbed the large brass doorknob. *We've been together so long.* James's mother and father were servants at the estate before he was born. *We had such fun as kids.* James closed the door and started walking toward the staircase at the far end of the hall. *The first time we were apart was when he went away to boarding school. He went on to Oxford to get his doctorate in economics and political governance, and then travelled the world after graduating. That was cut short when Prime Minister Chamberlain declared war on Germany in*—he hesitated at the base of the wide staircase trying to recall the month—*September 1939.* As he started up the stairs, he remembered the joy they experienced seeing each other again. *I joined the air force and Conrad worked in the London War Office and became a general. His unusual foresight resulted in many victories for Allied forces. He received several commendations.* Despite his heavy breathing, James's pace quickened slightly as he neared the top of the stairs. *When the war ended, we both came back to the estate and I've been his chauffeur ever since. Until three years ago, I drove him to The Club near 10 Downing Street every weekday morning at ten, and we went fox hunting or skeet shooting on Saturdays.*

James paused at the top of the stairs to take several deep breaths and recalled another, quite awkward, break in their close relationship. *He married in 1949. She was strikingly beautiful! An odd couple, she three inches taller.* His steps were thoughtfully slow as he started walking the long hallway. *I always avoided her, best I could. M'Lord pretended not to notice her flirtatious nature. She couldn't provide him with an heir, and he became discouraged with the marriage. Her death seemed to bother me more than him.* He took his handkerchief from the left back pocket of his pants and blew his nose. *After that he involved himself completely with worldly affairs, and Queen Elizabeth crowned him Lord Conrad in 1965.* As James lifted his loosely formed right fist, he thought, *There are so many things I want to ask him before*— He knocked twice and opened the door.

"Come in, James!" Lord Conrad shouted. "Where have you been?" He rolled to the side of the bed, swung thin bare white legs over, and planted his feet on the carpet. "The doctor gave me a clean bill of health." He wobbled as he stood and straightened the nightgown. His thin white hair was twisted in all directions. "I've got to get dressed for dinner. Get out my favourite duds, James, and tell Betsie to prepare duck and get out our favourite port. You and I are going to make a full night of it!"

Four hours later, the old friends walked side by side to one end of the long polished oak dining-room table. There were twenty Imperial period chairs around the table. The ceiling-to-floor drapes were closed. All the lights in the room were on, and two candelabra of lit full-length candles adorned the table. Conrad's eyes were bright with joy, his thin white hair was neatly plastered to his head and there was a surprising spring in his step. James towered over his master as he watched to ensure Conrad did not take a tumble. A small dish of salad greens had already been placed on each of the gold charger plates, and there were crystal glasses of water and port at each setting. Conrad's place was at the head of the table and James was to his right. James pulled Conrad's chair back, watched carefully as he sat down, and pushed the chair back toward the table before sitting down himself.

Conrad lifted the glass of port. "Cheers, my dear friend." He held the glass toward James.

James grabbed his glass. "Cheers to you, m'Lord. You are a dear friend and master." Glasses touched and they both listened as the pure crystalline sound demanded. They sipped the port in silence for a couple of minutes, then started eating. The salad tasted so good neither spoke a word until Betsie appeared.

"Hi, Betsie," Conrad almost shouted. "Lovely to see you. The salad was superb, as usual." He placed his salad fork on the empty plate.

James had followed Bestie's every move since she entered the room. He smiled at her as she removed his plate.

95

"Thankfully, Betsie is still with us," Conrad said after she left. He emptied his port glass. "What would we have done without her these past several years?"

"I agree, m'Lord." James's throat suddenly tightened at the thought of how he and Betsie secretly shared most evenings together. He quickly drained half his water glass, took a deep breath, and refilled their glasses of port.

"You know, James, I was just thinking that you and I have seen a lot of British history. Few others who are still alive today have been so fortunate."

"Yes, m'Lord. I remember almost everything since you and I went to war. The German bombing we endured, the victory celebrations, how busy you were advising Buckingham and Parliament how to rebuild and restructure our economy, the rebuilding efforts in the city, the troubles with Ireland, the great wealth from the oil discoveries in the North Sea, creation of the European Union, the great influx of immigrants from—"

"That's been very unfortunate," Conrad interrupted. He had never agreed with Britain's involvement in the European Union and was about to say something when Betsie walked in carrying two large plates of roast duck, carrots, dumplings, and mashed potatoes.

Betsie stood between them and leaned over to set the first plate in front of Lord Conrad. Her back was toward James. As per custom, James caressed her low on her right buttock with his left hand and, as she turned to the right to place his plate, his hand stayed on her leg. The oft-practiced routine continued as she reached her left hand over for the bottle of port and pushed hard against the resistance offered by James's hand. When she turned back to top up Conrad's glass, her soft sigh of pleasure was audible.

"What is it, Betsie?" Conrad looked up at her. "Are you okay?"

"Oh yes, m'Lord." There was joy in her voice. "Very well, thank you, m'Lord." She turned to fill James's port glass, winked at him as she placed the bottle back on the table, then turned and started walking toward the kitchen.

Conrad was already focused on enjoying his first mouthful of duck. "Mmmm, it's as good as ever, Betsie."

"Yes, m'Lord," she replied with a smile.

They ate in silence for a few minutes. Conrad could not remember when he had last enjoyed a meal so much. James's mind was bouncing back and forth between the uncontrollable expectation of spending another night with Betsie and the desire to clear up several questions that kept jumping in and out of his mind. He finally broke the silence. "A few things have been puzzling me, m'Lord, and I wonder if we could maybe discuss them."

Conrad finished chewing, swallowed, and reached for his glass of port. "Certainly, James. What's puzzling you?" He sipped the port, placed the glass back on the table, and had the knife and fork back in his hands before James answered.

"Well," James said slowly, "a few things; one related to the nine-eleven attack and—"

"What don't you understand about nine-eleven?" Conrad interrupted. "Speak frankly, James!"

"Yes, well, it's not really nine-eleven, so much as how you think different nations will react to it." He paused. "You always have such insight regarding things like that."

Conrad placed his knife and fork back on the plate, leaned back in the chair, and looked up at the ceiling in thought. "You know, James, that's a good question. We will support the Americans in whatever they want to do in dealing with that attack, because it was really the Americans who saved Britain in the two world wars. However, other nations aren't in quite the same position." As he paused to organize his thoughts he loaded his fork, filled his mouth, and chewed slowly. James gladly did the same.

"Canada's another story," Conrad finally continued. "I expect Canadians are both peed off and a little frightened, because some Americans, including many in the press, keep saying at least one of the terrorists entered the United States through Canada." He sipped his port. "As far as the United Nations and NATO are concerned, those nations will never come to a common agreement because there are just too many unknowns." Conrad seemed more interested in enjoying his meal than the subject at hand.

James swallowed and sipped his port without taking his eyes off Conrad. "I wonder most about Russia, China, and Israel."

"Those are easy assessments," Conrad said with a half-full mouth. He swallowed. "Israel will provide all sorts of advice and directions as to who to blame and what the Americans should do, but will never get directly involved with their own troops. China and Russia are most likely to stay completely out of it, and focus on preventing any direct involvement by the UN." He shrugged. "If the Americans invade any Eastern or Middle East nations without clearly proven cause, Russia or China, or both, could end up sending support, such as food and weapons and strategic advisers, to help those being invaded fend off the Americans." He shrugged again. "It's really not a clear picture, James, especially when there's not yet any proof who orchestrated the whole mess." His focus returned to eating.

"Thanks for your insight, m'Lord." James had almost cleared his plate. "One other thing is really bothering me."

Conrad was determined to finish his duck, mashed potatoes, and carrots before they got too cold. About ninety seconds went by before he asked, "So, James, what else is bothering you?"

"Yes, thank you, m'Lord." James was holding his empty port glass. "What I wonder is how Britain, how Germany—"

"Blurt it out, James, blurt it out!"

"How we lost so much of our influence and world power after winning the Second World War. How it is that Germany, who we defeated in that war, is now in control of the European Union and in cahoots with America on—"

"Damn, that looks good!" Conrad interrupted as he started another forkful of dumpling and potatoes toward his mouth.

"Heck," James continued as he reached for the bottle of port, "we had the greatest empire the world had ever known before that war started." He filled both their glasses and set the bottle back on the table. "We won the war, but for the past thirty or forty years we've had nothing but financial problems and some German or Swiss banker appointed by some other appointed people in the German-run European Union making judgements that have hollowed out all of our industrialization and created an open-ended inflow of immigrants who consume our social programs." He took a deep breath and grabbed his port glass.

There was a long silence as they both focused on their port and the morsels lingering on their plates. Conrad broke the silence. "I understand where you're coming from, James, but you know, we weren't the real winners of the Second World War. The real winners were the big European bankers." It was clear to James that he had hit a nerve and he tried to listen extra-closely as Conrad continued. "They hid in the shadows and influenced politicians from the peripheries while supplying the financing needed by all sides in the war. Those bankers made billions of pounds and dollars from the loans they made to governments and the companies making war machines and munitions." He paused. "World War Two was just part of a much bigger picture. Before that was the Russian Revolution and the First World War. During the Second World War, we became so indebted we had to sign a lend lease agreement that handed all our British naval bases to the Americans in exchange for their financial and oil support, and that transferred control of the world's oceans and international trade lanes over to them. Now? Well, those bankers have us and the whole American system by the balls." He took several seconds to recover his breath. "The stupidity of it all!" He grunted in disgust. "At least we were on the winning side long enough to see that history books were reasonably written."

James picked up on the reference. "You've written a great deal, m'Lord. Mostly about economics."

"You're right, James. After the War, I spent a lot of time and effort trying to explain how our government must maintain control over our economy. It is the fundamental responsibility of those who are democratically elected to our government to be the guardians of our capitalist society. They must ensure that all people living in our society benefit from the very robust nature of capitalism, and that the fundamental nature of capitalism is to provide jobs for all citizens who want to work and—," he grunted in disgust, "not simply for the benefit of banks, stock exchanges and the wealthy. I insisted the guardians must realize capitalism was conceived to open opportunities for the doers in society to get access to the nation's resources, for the purpose of benefitting all. I warned the guardians that they must pay close attention to ensure the system, while encouraging the capitalists, prevents them from becoming greedy and protects their enthusiasm from becoming prey for the money-lenders." Conrad paused. "We want aggressive business leaders and good jobs for our citizens. That's what capitalism is all about."

Many times, James had tried to understand Lord Conrad's writings but the theory of it all had always left him confused. "And, m'Lord, do you think those in government, those guardians, have done what you told them to do?"

"Maybe, for a while. But after Bretton Woods gave control of the IMF and World Bank to European bankers and the Zionists drove us out of Palestine, I became convinced that the guardians of our government were not paying proper attention to Britain's fundamental needs. About then, I started warning that a liberal press was not good for our nation because it spends too much time down-grading the capitalist ideals while sidetracking and challenging, rather than supporting and encouraging, our guardians." He reached for his glass of port. "But my warning fell on deaf ears, and look what we've got now!" He quickly took two swigs. "My father used to say the Roman Empire created a Western world based on solid Christian ethics and morals, and our British Empire was an unwitting participant in the destruction of those ethics and morals because the guardians of our system got all wrapped up in the secular initiatives of the Masonic movement, and made the mistake of endorsing a free press that equated democratic freedom with liberalism." He took a deep breath and let it out in frustration. "My father knew what he was talking about."

James swallowed hard. "He was a fine man, but I still don't understand."

"Few really do. Few even give a damn. That's the problem today. People don't care about the past, or even the future for that matter! But they should." He emptied his glass and pushed it across the table toward James. "Top that up for me, James."

James grabbed the bottle and filled the glass while Conrad continued talking. "Christian societies became too liberal. I remember father telling me the Zionists knew how to run a nation properly. 'Just watch what they do in Israel,' he told me after they drove us out of there." Conrad gave the table a couple of hard raps with the handle end of his fork. "He said the Zionists would govern strictly by their protocols and never allow religion any meaningful influence in Palestine. He said they would keep their people working, control their own money supply, and never praise a press that goes overboard with liberal views. Father was convinced zero-sum leadership would eventually make Israel the greatest nation in the world." He began to choke.

"What is it, m'Lord?"

Conrad cleared his throat. "Nothing, James, nothing. I was just remembering how father believed the only way to prevent another world war was to ensure Israel never got military aircraft and weapons—" He started coughing and took a moment to steady himself. "And to ensure Egypt remained the only military powerhouse in that part of the world."

He's not to get excited! James reached over and pushed Conrad's water glass toward him while offering the only consolation that came to his mind. "Well, the Bible says—"

"Bah!" Conrad exclaimed as his face became redder and redder. He took a deep breath and threw his arms toward the ceiling in frustration, just as Betsie entered from the kitchen. She jumped sideways as the fork flew out of Conrad's hand and past her ear on its way to the floor.

She quickly topped up the glasses of port and gathered the empty dishes. "Would you like dessert and coffee now, m'Lord?"

Conrad's face had turned chalk white. "Later, Betsie, later. Please leave us now."

Betsie picked the fork up from the floor as she left the room.

James was frightened for his master. "M'Lord, I remember when your father got so enraged about the politics of our country that he died of a heart attack." He said it as softly as he could in an effort to quiet Conrad, but it seemed to make things worse.

"That happened because our troops left Palestine in 1947," Conrad almost shouted. "It left the Zionists in control." He gulped for air. "Father called it one of the worst decisions Britain ever made. The whole Middle East has been a hotbed of trouble ever since." He looked at James and pounded his right fist on the table. "James, that's another thing I've been writing about over these past years." His face, neck, and hands were chalk white. "Our Western world should be peaceful and safe. The people in our nations should be secure under the moral base of a strong and unconfused Christian religion, without great debt, properly educated and not confused by the media at every turn, speaking common languages in our schools, governments with strong guardians, productive and proud in our work and our families, living in peaceful societies." His voice was hoarse and so low James could barely hear. "Not living under rules made by officials who are helplessly confused by liberalized media and economic theories invented by unaccountable and poorly regulated bankers. Each nation should have control of its own wealth."

To Conrad, it seemed that he was back in time, addressing the House of Commons in the British Parliament. His voice became loud.

"Trade between nations should be controlled by the guardians our citizens elect to government, not by corporations with owners hiding in the shadows, living outside the country, and avoiding proper taxes. Our nation must control its own borders!" He took a deep breath. "The guardians we choose to lead our nation must have great character, character such as that so beautifully described by Rudyard Kipling, in his poem, "If". You all know the poem well; can you just imagine what it would read like if Kipling had tried to include characteristics reflected by those who expound and demand the virtues of gay rights, alternate lifestyles, open borders, and all the rest of the nonsense we're forced to deal with today?" He roared with serious laughter. "If we expect Britain to ever be great again," Conrad sensed he was in his prime and speaking to the leaders of Britain, "we must support our guardians, and the first action they must take is to get us the hell out of the European—" Lord Conrad slumped forward and his head slammed face down on the gold charger plate, dead.

James just sat there, bewildered. The glass of port fell from his hand and shattered on the table. "Betsie! HELP!" he finally shouted.

Betsie was standing at the kitchen door with two bowls of vanilla ice cream, caramel sauce, and crushed walnuts, her mouth open and unable to move or speak.

STORY 3

PALESTINE & ISRAEL

CHAPTER 8

BOYS OF WEST JERUSALEM

Fifty-four years earlier
April 1947; West Jerusalem

On April 2, 1947, the British government, weary of the struggle of governing the mandated Jewish homeland in Palestine, informed the United Nations it would give up its mandate and asked the UN General Assembly to make recommendations concerning the future government of Palestine. The United Nations Special Committee on Palestine published its report on August 31, 1947. The report proposed that Palestine be partitioned into two sovereign states, one Jewish and the other Arab. Jerusalem would be given to neither state but would form a demilitarized and neutralized city with international trusteeship and a governor under the United Nations; Jerusalem's governor was to be neither an Arab nor a Jew, nor a citizen of the new Arab or Jewish states. The Jewish Agency for Palestine accepted the plan, but many Zionists, notably the Irgun and Stern/Lehi gangs, opposed it and violence increased in the area. The Arab Higher Committee refused to accept the partitioning of the country, demanding instead an independent Palestinian state under Palestinian-Arab rule from the Mediterranean to the Jordan.

"I don't like the boys pretending to be Irgun fighters!" Shelley Ha-am said as she twisted the ends of her long, thick, wavy black hair in the thin fingers of her right hand.

It was early November 1947. Shelley and Anna Kahane were having tea and watching their two five-year-old boys as they played in the front street outside Anna's home. The ladies had met at the hospital five years earlier after giving birth to their sons and their friendship had grown. Both wore long dresses patterned in soft-coloured floral designs.

"Things are getting worse, Anna! Now the Irgun and Lehi are killing Jews, not just the British and Arabs." Shelley kept twisting her hair, and her dark eyes blinked nervously. "They're dividing our people." After moving from England to Palestine in 1918, Shelley's parents had followed David Ben-Gurion and helped establish a kibbutz near Tel Aviv where Shelley was born and trained in the Hebrew tradition. She and her pharmacist husband had lost two children during pregnancies before being blessed with Simon. "Why are those thugs our children's heroes?"

Anna tried to be sympathetic. "That's just how boys are, Shelley." Anna was a large woman with a podgy, lightly tanned face, large lips, and frizzy light-brown, sun-bleached hair ending just below colourful earrings. She knew little of her parents' backgrounds; only that they had lived in the Pale of Russia before joining in the Aliyah to the new Jewish homeland in 1919. Chaim was the youngest of her four healthy and robust children, and Anna was convinced that, despite her marriage to a simple tailor man, the Almighty had used her as a modest source of future greatness for the Jewish homeland. "I don't understand, either. Just the other day, Shalom Gurewitz was killed because he was a member of the British Criminal Investigation Department. He was a good person, a good Jew."

"Why don't the authorities remove the terrorist gangs?" Shelley's voice was unusually forceful. "They should be sent back where they came from. To Russia, Poland, Germany—wherever they came from."

Anna was surprised that she half agreed with Shelley. She refocused on the children. "Don't worry, my dear. Boys will be boys. They'll soon work it out of their system."

On November 29, 1947, the United Nations voted on the partition resolution. It was passed with thirty-three votes in favour, thirteen against, with ten abstentions. The abstentions included Great Britain. The opponents included six Arab and four other Muslim states. Both the United States and the Soviet Union voted in favour. The Arab Higher Committee immediately called for a three-day general strike and a complete boycott on the purchase of all Jewish goods, and it seemed the fabric of Jerusalem was about to disintegrate.

On December 5, the Jewish Agency announced the call-up of all men and women between the ages of seventeen and twenty-five for national military service. The Haganah, which had been formed by Vladimir Jabotinsky in 1920 and was still illegally armed, took over responsibility for the defence of Jews against attacks from Arabs.

Several months later
May 1948

"No, Simon, you and Chaim cannot go outside and play." Shelley stared down at her son. There was innocence in Simon's dark eyes as he looked up at his mother. He had been wrestling with Chaim and his curly black hair was twisted in all directions. Chaim stood behind Simon, taller, stronger, his curlier black hair still neatly combed, and his dark eyes bright with anticipation that Simon would be able to talk his mother into letting them go outside to play freedom fighters.

Shelley thumped the palms of her hands down on the kitchen table and glared at Simon. "There will be no freedom fighter war games around here. Show Chaim how well you play your violin. Go now, and play quietly."

The boys turned and headed to Simon's bedroom. Shelley turned to Anna, who was sitting across the table. "This is awful. The violence is increasing. We're afraid to walk the streets of our city. Why have the British pulled their troops out? They were to stay until September." She answered her own question. "They couldn't afford any more deaths." She threw her arms in the air. "It's gone on for too long." She paused, swallowed, and started twisting the ends of her hair. "I'm afraid our people are as much to blame as the Arabs."

"No, Shelley, it's the Arab terrorists." The tone of Anna's voice suggested a new impatience. "For six months now they have killed our people. We must do something."

On May 14, 1948, Jewish leaders proclaimed the State of Israel. Armed forces of Egypt, Transjordan, Syria, Lebanon, and Iraq attacked Israel the next day. The resulting battle became known as the War of Independence. Zionist leaders had planned well. On May 20, some five hundred airmen arrived from the United States and Canada and became part of the new Israeli Air Force that was using aircraft acquired as surplus equipment after WWII. It was the turning point in the war. By the end of May, the invading Arab nations were on the run. On June 11, the Jews and Arabs signed a ceasefire that had been called for by the United Nations Security Council.

Late in June 1948, United Nations mediator Count Bernadotte produced a plan proposing that Jerusalem become part of an Arab State, with King Abdullah of Transjordan as sovereign. Israel's provisional government, meeting in Tel Aviv, rejected the plan and any other changes to the previous United Nations resolution. The Arabs refused to extend the ceasefire and fighting was renewed throughout Palestine. The Israeli government proclaimed the areas of Jerusalem that were under its control to be Israeli-occupied territories. Count Bernadotte's efforts to establish a permanent peace were rejected. On September 17, 1948, Bernadotte's car was ambushed by members of the Lehi Gang; Bernadotte and a French army officer in the car were murdered.

By the end of 1948, more than 700,000 Palestinians had been expelled from the lands claimed by Israel, the British police and military were gone, the Haganah had taken over peacekeeping responsibility, and the citizens of Israel sensed peace was at hand.

David Ben-Gurion, the first prime minister of the new State of Israel, quickly merged the three Jewish fighting forces that had frequently operated with conflicting agendas. Vladimir Jabotinski's Haganah was given the police and military leadership for the new state, and the Irgun and Lehi gangs were quickly brought under the Haganah umbrella. Zionist agents had been busy clandestinely amassing arms and military equipment from the United States, Canada, Western Europe, and Czechoslovakia; the Haganah's initial war chest included three B-17 bombers, some C-46 transport planes, several half-track vehicles, 65-mm French mountain guns, 120-mm mortars, H-35 light tanks, twenty-five Avia S-199 fighter planes, hundreds of heavy machine guns, a limitless supply of light rifles, and millions of rounds of ammunition. The State of Israel was ready to defend itself.

"Thank goodness the boys can play safely outside again," Shelley said as she poured Anna another cup of tea. It had been almost a year since Ben-Gurion took Israel to statehood.

"The armistice with Egypt and the shift of our capital city to Jerusalem has made a big difference, no matter what the United Nations says or thinks," Anna agreed. "We all feel safer. We'll be a great nation someday. We can now live in peace."

Seven years later

In 1956, Egypt nationalized the Suez Canal and restricted passage of ships destined to Israel. Encouraged by Britain and France, Israeli forces invaded Egypt on October 29, 1956. During the battle, Egypt completely blocked the canal by intentionally sinking forty ships, and the Suez Canal Crisis followed. A truce agreement was finally arranged under the auspices of the United Nations, and the Canal was reopened in March 1957; however, Israel refused to give up the land it had taken in Gaza, and a war of attrition resulted.

The boys were fourteen at the start of the Suez Crisis. Chaim could hardly wait to reach seventeen and become eligible for military service. They often argued about the plight of Palestinians who, once almost their friends, were now refugees. "I wonder where they're living?" Simon once said. "Who gives a shit?" Chaim immediately reacted. "They're in Gaza, or the West Bank, or Jordan, or Syria, or Lebanon. Who gives a shit, Simon? Just as long as they never come back here!"

Whenever Shelley and her pharmacist husband discussed Simon's future, she would say, "We must send him to America so he can safely study music and become a great violinist."

CHAPTER 9

FIGHT OR PERISH

Simon was sixteen when his parents sent him to live with his aunt and uncle in New York City in the spring of 1958. He enrolled at the Juilliard School of Music that fall, but his fingers were too small to handle advanced demands of the violin and he dropped out following his second year of study. The next year, he enrolled in the pre-medical college at Columbia University. In 1963, soon after acceptance into the medical college, he married a nurse and they lived in a small apartment owned by her father in north Manhattan.

Four years later, Israel achieved a crushing victory over the Arab nations in the Six Day War. The victory completely transformed feelings within the Jewish community in New York. The jubilation went on for weeks. Simon learned from his mother's letters that Chaim had contributed significantly to the victory. His father-in-law repeatedly insisted, "It's of paramount importance for all American Jews to support and feel great pride in Israel." When classes started that fall, Simon's heart was no longer in medicine. He transferred to the college of political science and discovered a new passion.

Simon's political science studies involved keeping close watch on all Israeli developments, including the problematic growth and influence of Yasser Arafat's Palestine Liberation Organization. He excelled in his studies and was granted a doctorate degree in 1972. The next year, he accepted a junior professorship in the Political Science College at Columbia University.

Israel

Chaim had no interest in extending his education beyond the minimum required. On his seventeenth birthday, he joined the army and excelled during the training program. In 1960, he was assigned to an armored tank division responsible for defending Israel's northern borders with Lebanon and Syria. He had been in the military for seven years when Israeli forces successfully pulled off the surprise pre-emptive attack against all neighbouring Arab nations in June 1967. Under the leadership of General Moshe Dayan, Israel's combined air and ground forces took only six days to destroy military facilities and operations in Egypt, Syria, and Jordan. The victory gave Israel control over the West Bank, Golan Heights, Gaza, the Sinai Peninsula, and the whole of Palestine. Pressures on Chaim's military responsibilities mounted in 1969 after Yasser Arafat became leader of the Palestine Liberation Organization.

Initially, the PLO primarily represented Palestinian refugees living in the West Bank and Jordan. However, the breadth of Arafat's influence broadened when the Jordanian government expelled hundreds of thousands of Palestinian refugees to United Nations camps in southern Lebanon in 1970, and those refugees created increased tensions along Israel's northern border.

New York

"Simon! Simon!" It was October 6, 1973. Simon's wife was shaking him out of a deep sleep. "Wake up, Simon. Something terrible—"

Simon was looking into eyes of panic. "What is it!?" He looked at the bedside clock. *Only six-thirty.*

"Israel is being destroyed! The Arabs invaded hours ago!" Panic filled her voice. "And—"

"It's Yom Kippur," Simon said. *Nothing is to happen on Yom Kippur!* He sat up in bed. "What can we do?"

"Nothing, except pray!"

Yom Kippur is holiest day of the year in Judaism, a time to refrain from work, to fast, to attend synagogue services, and to atone for the sins of the past year. It's a time to refrain from washing and bathing, anointing one's body, wearing leather shoes, and engaging in sex; it's a day to be dedicated to prayer. Egyptian, Syrian, Jordanian, and Iraqi military forces had launched a surprise attack when Israel's guard was down. Egyptian forces overwhelmed Israeli forces in Gaza, Syrian tank divisions took control of the Golan Heights, Jordan attacked on the West Bank, and Iraqi fighter jets and soldiers supported the invasion. Jews in America were glued to their radios.

"The battle has turned!" Simon's father-in-law declared at dinner on the fourth day. "America has saved our homeland."

Washington politicians and the Pentagon had reacted immediately, with more than five hundred air shipments of advanced munitions and equipment to Israel and a continuous American air surveillance that helped pinpoint the locations of attacking Arab forces. By the fourth day, the Israeli military was turning the battle. In the south, Israeli forces drove the Egyptians out of the Sinai, captured the Suez Canal, and advanced toward Cairo. In the north and east, Israel recaptured the West Bank and Golan Heights, and drove to within thirty-five miles of the Syrian capital of Damascus before a ceasefire sponsored by the United Nations brought fighting to an end on October 24. Following the ceasefire, Israel disengaged from the Suez Canal but kept control over Sinai.

The war shook America's Jewish communities to the core. Simon and his wife were discussing things at dinner in late October. "Moshe Dayan and Prime Minister Meir were careless," she said. "Daddy says Mossad had warned that something was in the wind. He says we Jews can never let our guards down, not even on the holiest of days. He says Golda Meir and Moshe Dayan must resign. He says Israel will always need to fight, or it will perish."

"Dayan should fall on his sword," Simon agreed, "to save the prime minister and the Labour party."

"Daddy says it's time for Likud to take over."

"I'm not sure," Simon said. "Washington must insist upon a lasting peace settlement, not more wars."

The Yom Kippur War was significant for America because Arab nations immediately introduced an oil embargo against the United States and its allies. Simon's father-in-law laughed. "Americans don't care what the Arabs do, Simon. We will endure any hardships for Israel's sake."

"Maybe," Simon said. "But if the oil embargo lasts too long it could seriously impact the U.S. economy, and might have an influence on world affairs lasting for generations."

"Ah." His father-in-law brushed it off. "You have no idea about these things. Relax."

Simon continued his professorship at Columbia and became an adviser to the White House administration when President Carter mediated peace negotiations between Israel's Prime Minister Begin and Egypt's President Sadat in 1979. The experience broadened his understanding of America's policies in relation to Israel and the Islamic nations.

"Will you advise President Reagan?" his wife wondered as they watched the January 1981 television coverage of Reagan's swearing-in ceremony.

"That depends on how the president and his administration decide to deal with Israel and the rest of the Middle East," Simon replied. A month later, he was thanked for his past service and told there was no need for him to be involved.

A few months later
Israel

"WE DID IT!" Chaim shouted to the walls of a small empty office in Mossad headquarters. *YES!!* He pounded his fist hard on the desk.

It was June 7, 1981, and Chaim had just cradled the telephone after hearing that all F-15 interceptors and F-16 fighter bombers were safe and on their way back to Israel after a successful mission to destroy Iraq's nuclear power plant near Baghdad. Chaim had been assigned to the Mossad in 1980, and he was a member of the strategy team that planned every aspect of the pre-emptive bombing mission. Destruction of Iraq's Osirak nuclear facility would be another feather in his cap.

Prime Minister Begin will be very pleased. He fired his right fist into the air and repeated, "WE DID IT!" Chaim felt the power and adventure of being associated with Mossad and its clandestine affairs, and he realized that his training program was the first step in becoming part of an efficient, effective, and brutal international spy network that could become the envy of the world.

New York

Simon's graduate class at the Political Science College of Columbia University was deeply entrenched in studying Israel's military achievements. Studies also included how Zionist political theory and objectives were impacting the development of that nation. By mid-1982, those studies had expanded to include the purpose and practicality of the United Nations as it related to Israel's development.

Late that year, Simon lectured, "The world needs to accept that Israel is a Zionist nation, the only one in the world. Other people and nations will never be able to seriously influence how Israel is governed. It will be governed only by Zionist rules. Voting and decisions at the United Nations can only peripherally affect the direction of Israel. The fact is, many other nations would do well to learn from Israel and operate with a similar self-centred focus to ensure the safety, security, welfare, purity of belief, and long-term solidarity of their own citizens." He was purposely cautious in any criticism of U.S. policy directions at the United Nations. "Yes, I agree," he reacted to a question from a student. "It may be puzzling when our president and congressional leaders criticize Israel's actions in Palestine and, at the same time, use America's veto power at the UN Security Council to prevent UN efforts to stop Israeli operations in the Occupied Territories and Lebanon. But Washington has its reasons for these things."

In December 1985, a month after Jonathan and Anne Pollard were arrested by the FBI for several years of passing top secret military information to Israel through the Israeli Embassy in Washington, Chaim was assigned to diplomatic work in that embassy. Before leaving for Washington, he met with the Pollards' handler and was told, "The Pollards taught us a lesson, Chaim. If a spy of ours ever again runs to our embassy for asylum, shoot him in the head and deny everything."

While in Washington, Chaim assisted the Anti-Defamation League and other pro-Israel groups to turn the focus of the American people away from the Pollard Affair and toward support of a multi-million-dollar U.S. loan Prime Minister Shamir could use to create homes for tens of thousands of Soviet Jews immigrating to the Occupied Territories. Each time he visited New York, he thought of his old friend. *I must avoid any chance of running into Simon; he's persona non grata.*

Simon was becoming more and more obsessed with Washington's apparent unqualified support of Likud activities in Palestine. The final straw occurred in 1987 when he concluded in one of his lectures, "Likud's militaristic aggressions in the Occupied Territories have prompted a Palestinian Intifada movement and a declaration by Hamas that it will never recognize the State of Israel. Washington has got to take action, support UN efforts to end brutalities in the territories, and finally bring peace to the whole region."

Word of Simon's remark quickly spread within New York's Jewish community. On Friday evening, his father-in-law called and invited him to meet him at his club for lunch the next day.

They were in a private room, just the two of them. It was family talk while they ate, during which his father-in-law made a point of stressing how proud he was of Simon's two sons and the way his daughter and Simon had parented the boys. The plates had been cleared and they were having a second cup of coffee when his father-in-law looked into his eyes.

"Simon, you've become a fine teacher, a dedicated and learned man in your profession." He paused briefly. "I was visited by a wise and important man yesterday, one of WJC's New York leaders. He has followed your career at Columbia and is impressed by your teaching abilities, and your interest in current events in Israel." Another brief pause. "He asked me to tell you that WJC wants you to move to Jerusalem and teach at the university there."

Simon felt shocked. There was a long silence. "What about my family?" His voice cracked on the last word.

"Of course, son. Your family will move to Jerusalem with you. You will have a fine situation there."

Simon cleared his throat. His cheeks were red. "Why is the World Jewish Congress involved? Am I free to—"

"Of course. We're always free to follow our own desires—within the law, of course." He paused. "Thankfully, America is a nation of clearly defined laws." Another pause. "Civic laws, state laws, federal laws. They all have a special place and purpose, and each of those jurisdictions have courts of judges to interpret the laws." His voice was filled with confidence and compassion. "The WJC is blessed with a council of the most learned men, and those men have been able to ensure we operate effectively within American laws, without attracting past prejudices. To have the attention of those learned men is truly a blessing." It was clear to him that Simon was far from convinced. "Those men can make great things happen, son. You should consider it a real honour to have their attention and advice regarding your future."

I've no choice, Simon thought. He wondered how serious things really were. "The WJC contacted you directly?"

"Yes, that's right. I'm sure you're aware both the WJC and its Executive Committee are headquartered here in New York." He sounded matter-of-fact and encouraging. "You've had the attention of some very important men."

Simon was in a daze after he left his father-in-law and walked from the Club to the subway. He was oblivious of the people standing around him on the train. *I shouldn't have been so critical of the Likud. They will control my teaching in Israel. Maybe I'm fortunate!* He tried to recall what he knew of the World Jewish Congress. *It originated in Geneva in 1936, an international federation of Jewish communities and organizations to deal with the Nazi onslaught in Germany. Its base was the World Zionist Organization and it quickly developed representation throughout the Western world, including Russia. No question, without the WJC, world Jewry may not have survived WWII.* Suddenly new thoughts struck him. *Why did the WJC continue after the war ended? To ensure Jewish patriotism toward Israel and Zionism? To gain special Jewish influence in other nations? To control world Jewry?* Unsettling thoughts and questions were racing through his mind. *I know nothing of WJC's moral base and governing philosophies.* He took deep breathes in an effort to relieve a tightening in his chest. *I feel locked-in, not free.* The train stopped. He looked out the window to read the station sign. *One more stop.* He checked the time on his wrist-watch. As the train started moving, another issue popped into his mind. *My family is Jewish American. Being part of a world-wide tribe has never entered my mind, until now!* He pondered his options. *Really, I don't have an option!* As the train started, he prepared himself to get off at the next stop and greet his family with the news. *They need to believe I'm anxious to teach in Jerusalem. Mother will sure be pleased.*

A month later
1987; Jerusalem

Shelley Ha-am and Anna Kahane sat at the small table in the kitchen of Shelley's home in Jerusalem. Both ladies were in their late sixties. Each of their husbands had died in the early 1980s. Anna had gained weight, her frizzy white hair was thin, and her eyes had lost their intensity. Shelley looked vibrant and healthy, and her eyes were bright with anticipation.

"I have a surprise, Anna," Shelley said as she poured tea into Anna's cup.

Anna's head jerked up and her tongue flicked across her lips. "What is it?"

Shelley filled her own cup and put the teapot on the stand. "Simon is coming home," she said. "He's coming back to Jerusalem to teach political science at the university. His family will be with him; his wife and two boys. I've seen their pictures but we've never met. I'm so excited!"

Anna felt strangely deflated. "Why is he coming back here?" There was an uncomfortable tone in her voice.

"He plans to help our nation," Shelley answered proudly. "He believes we can live peacefully with the Palestinians and all Arabs."

Anna rolled her eyes and reached for her tea cup. *Impossible! Simon has become stupid. We're surrounded by more and more Arab terrorism each day!* "Wouldn't that be nice," she said. *Chaim will not be happy!*

CHAPTER 10

GAME CHANGER: A TERRIFYING IDEA

The same week
June 1987; Qatar

It was late morning on a blistering hot day in June 1987. Dense, high-humidity air drifting inland from the Persian Gulf blocked the direct sunlight and partially camouflaged the large white tent at the end of a temporary road on the deserted coast of Qatar. Condensed water formed in heavy droplets on the outside of the tent and on each of several Rolls Royce limousines parked in front of the structure with motors running and air conditioners on. There was a driver in each car. Inside the tent were tables configured in a circle, as if for a meeting of the United Nations Security Council. However, neither the United Nations nor any other governing organization in the world knew of this gathering of the twenty most senior imams in the Middle East and Africa with the tall, thin, dark-haired, lightly bearded forty-five-year-old Palestinian who stood at the head table.

Ammad Bashara had been standing quietly for almost thirty minutes, surveying the gathering as each religious leader entered the tent and took his place as designated by nameplates on the tables. There were several nods of recognition and respect but no one spoke. The imams were dressed in religious garments, Ammad in a sparkling white, ankle-length *dishdashah* shirt and a white *ghutrah* headcloth held in place by a black *agal* ring. A large bottle of water and a glass were at each setting.

Ammad smiled respectfully as the last imam took his seat. "Praise to Allah." He spoke in a language well known to all the attendees. His voice was deeper and more powerful than one might expect. "Allah has blessed this gathering. May He give me the strength and wisdom to clearly follow His guidance and deliver His message with proper respect, humility, clarity, meaning, and direction."

The imams were all familiar with Ammad's background. He was born in a humble home on a narrow winding street near the Temple Mount in East Jerusalem in 1942. His parents, both brilliant scholars and school teachers, had prayed that the last of their five children would be a boy. In many ways, Ammad seemed an ordinary Palestinian child, participating with his four sisters and many friends in early childhood activities. He was almost six when his parents became obsessed with the great catastrophe, *nakba*. They sensed a spiritual change in Ammad, which, along with the increasing levels of anti-Palestinian activities, convinced his father to move his family out of danger. They moved to Jordan in late 1951, and within a couple of years, Ammad's Jordanian teachers all agreed he was special. As one said, "It is clear that Ammad is wrapped in the Prophet's spiritual quilt." When he turned fourteen, the king of Jordan encouraged special tutoring for the boy and eventually arranged for him to be trained in the best schools and universities of the world. Ammad's advanced studies covered many details of the social, religious, and economic aspects of Western societies. By the time he was thirty, he was fluent in several languages, and had a deep knowledge of international affairs and the economic objectives and theories of most political systems. He was thirty-one and attending the final year of doctorate studies in International Relations at Cambridge University when the Arab nations attacked Israel on Yom Kippur in 1973. His subsequent doctorate thesis was a rambling outline of the potential long-term consequences of the oil weapon imposed by Arab nations after losing the war, and a warning: "The people of the Book (Arabs, Christians, and Jews) must eliminate radial elements of their societies if they are to live in peace." He spent several years presenting his thesis throughout the Islamic world. However, when the United Nations failed to condemn and penalize Israel after it invaded Iraq and destroyed that nation's nuclear power plant in early June '81, Ammad lost faith in the practicality of his thesis. This meeting in Qatar was designed to push beyond direct confrontation and refocus all Islam on a new initiative.

"These words from Allah," he continued. "Six years ago today, Satan's terrorist network struck with a surprise bombing of Iraq's nuclear power facility. It was the beginning of a new and bold initiative by the Zionists who hide behind our Jewish brothers and deep in the shadows of American and British financial and political power. For too many years, since *nakba* in 1948, Arab nations have been unable to act effectively as one against the Zionist devil. It is time for change!"

He paused for a drink. Many imams shifted, coughed, and looked around anxiously.

"Allah has disclosed a strategy. Nothing of our preparation is to be written—ever! We must carefully memorize our plans and strategies. The plan will require us to do things that are not in the true nature of Allah's teachings."

Coughing, serious head-scratching, and nervous shuffling broke the silence. A few imams glanced at each other with puzzled frowns. Most eyes were fixed on Ammad in uneasy anticipation.

"It would be fatal to undertake a direct economic or military battle against Satan's regime at this time. Our defensive jihad must be subtle, undetectable, and designed to effectively drive the enemy from the Middle East so that, many years from now, peaceful caliphates may operate within our lands."

For the next four hours, the religious leaders memorized the protocols Ammad delivered to them. They were simple, organized under five key initiatives: 1) Islamic population expansion and dispersion, 2) Islamic footprint expansion, 3) attracting Western money, military training, and weaponry, 4) maintaining Western dependence on Middle East hydrocarbons, and 5) an intelligence network in the West.

"With Allah's blessing, I will contact each of you monthly," Ammad concluded after all had adequately grasped and memorized the protocols. "At those times, we will ensure our protocols remain precise in our memories and that we maintain confidence in the ability to implement the necessary programs. No one else is to know these protocols exist. I will ensure that, upon any of your deaths, your successor is immediately brought into this fold." He made eye contact with most of the imams. "Each of you will now encourage development of your nation's own programs. You each must ensure complete secrecy because the strategy will bring your nations into conflict with each other. There are sure to be terrible wars, both civil and international. The current conflicts between Iran and Iraq and in Afghanistan are ideal beginnings, a perfect starting point. Although there will be many deaths, the conflicts will harden and strengthen our people and our nations and will eventually, many decades from now, put us in a position to effectively bring our forces together as one in victory."

Ammad said nothing for over a minute as he focused on their eyes to seek the necessary pact of assurance.

"This program must never be disclosed," he repeated in a firm and confident voice. "I will remain close to each of you and your programs. I will create the intelligence network necessary to bind, conduct, and protect our program. In time, many of our people will become exceptionally well-equipped, well-trained, and great leaders—morally, strategically, and militarily. They will be capable of effectively leading Allah's ultimate battle against Satan's horde. I assure you, our Jewish and Christian brothers throughout the Western nations will join us in the battle once they finally grasp how the Zionists have so skilfully used them as puppets and pawns during past millennia.

"We must have a secret code that is known only to ourselves. We shall state that code three times in succession, from both directions, before speaking to each other. If that is not done, be assured the one speaking to you is a fake. The code will be *Arab Spring*. I repeat, it must be expressed three times by each party to the conversation." He paused. "Like this: Arab Spring, Arab Spring, Arab Spring." He smiled. "May Allah be with us all, and may Allah bless each of you and your people."

Ammad turned and walked from the tent. As he settled into the back seat of the waiting limousine, he thought, *Patience is critical. The first step, a major increase in birth rate and an education boom to open youthful minds to radical thoughts, will take many years.* A smile crossed his lips. *With the Islamic Brotherhood, Hezbollah, and Hamas, we've got a good start. Allahu Akbar!*

CHAPTER 11

WILL THINGS NEVER CHANGE?

Twelve years later
November 1999; Jerusalem

It was mid-afternoon on a bright and sunny mid-week day. Simon's pace was brisk as he walked up the front steps to the Political Science building at the Hebrew University of Jerusalem. He was the head of the university's Political Science faculty and one of the most respected professors on campus.

It had been nearly a dozen years since Simon and his father-in-law had their fateful meeting at the Club in Manhattan. From the front steps of the Club, his father-in-law had watched Simon dejectedly shuffle down the street toward the subway station, and realized his daughter's family could be in serious trouble unless he did something to ensure Simon's future in Israel was handled with great care. He spent the next few weeks in meetings with WJC leaders and prepping his daughter. When the family arrived in Israel, the red carpet was out. The university had arranged for Simon's mother to lead a group in greeting the new arrivals at the Tel Aviv Airport. For over thirty minutes there was great joy, love, and tears in the arrival lounge. The university president handed Simon a four-day itinerary that was designed to keep him busy, and ensure the family was quickly settled into a fine three-bedroom home in a respected West Jerusalem neighbourhood. During the following days, the teen-age boys were registered in school and welcomed by new classmates, the family met leaders at the local synagogue, and Simon was welcomed into a fraternity of colleagues with open arms as a senior professor in Political Science at Hebrew University of Jerusalem. The week was quite overwhelming, pleasurable, and encouraging for the whole family, and could only have happened through the focused dedication of his father-in-law and an exceptionally capable and close-knit Jewish community. The family settled into new routines with ease, and the next eleven years were filled with many pleasures, and some significant changes. The boys both graduated from university, the oldest in Economics and his younger brother in Business Finance. They married sisters they had met in their Jerusalem high school and, just a year ago, in the summer of 1998, both had moved to New York where they began working on Wall Street in a firm owned by their uncles, their mother's two younger brothers. Simon and his wife had never returned to New York; but they often enjoyed looking at pictures of the city sent with weekly letters, and searching for any signs that a baby Ha-am might be on the way.

Simon nodded toward the full class of Political Science students as he walked to the lectern. His grey suit hung a bit baggy from his shoulders and hips. His long, curly hair was thick and heavily greyed, but his eyes sparkled with interest and enthusiasm.

"Okay, who wants to be first?" he scanned the class. "Your assignment was to assume you're nearing the end of your second term as the president of the United States. You're concerned about the country's dependence upon OPEC oil, you're frustrated with the lack of success in your personal efforts to sponsor a meaningful and lasting Middle East peace, you're accused of infidelity, and the American economy threatens to go deeper in debt. What would you do?"

Several hands were raised. Simon smiled. "I'm glad to see your enthusiasm." He pointed. "Ehud, you first. What would you do if you were President Clinton and—?"

Windows shattered and a tidal wave of broken glass tore through flesh and clothing as it swept across the classroom. The force of the explosion pinned Simon's back against the blackboard while glass punctured his clothes, face, and hands. Everyone was screaming. Simon took bleeding hands from his face and looked out at a demolished classroom of hysterical students.

"Stay calm," he yelled. "Stay calm and help each other."

The scene was soon under police control. The suicide bombers had died in a van loaded with explosives, nails, and other shrapnel in front of the university administration building, next to the political science building. Anyone within a twenty-metre radius of the van was either dead or seriously injured. Simon's classroom was just outside the kill zone, but many of his students were injured and seriously traumatized.

That evening, Simon and his wife watched a televised report of the attack. "The terrorists were Palestinian students," the journalist reported. "Police haven't determined how the bomb-loaded van got onto campus without detection. It all happened quickly. Police and government authorities are pointing at Fatah. Our independent sources indicate it could have been Hamas." The reporter paused as a paper was handed to him. "We've just been advised that Hezbollah is claiming credit for the attack." He coughed. "The university will be closed until authorities complete their investigation." The televised picture showed police searching through the shattered wreckage of the administration building.

Simon grabbed the remote and hit the off button. He had small bandages on his forehead, left cheek, and the backs of his hands.

"We should go to bed, honey." His wife stood and held out her hands to help him up from the chair.

As he stood, he looked into her eyes. "You know, dear, I'm really puzzled. Palestinians may have good reason to hate us, but the great depth of determination in their impossible cause is a puzzle to me. Those who carried out the attack were considered exceptional students."

They were walking to the bedroom. "I know. Sometimes it seems the whole world is against us." She shrugged. "Why are we always the centre of so much anger?"

It took Simon a while to answer. "That very thought may be part of the problem," he said. "We don't seem able to stop believing others hate us. And yet, it's been so many years, and we've accomplished so much."

"What do you mean?" she asked.

"Today, our country leads the world, all other countries, in medical and other scientific research. Our teachings and focus on the history of mankind are unparalleled. Maybe it's that knowledge of history that makes us feel hated." He shrugged. "A week ago, one of my students asked why we have such a zero-sum mentality and never offer olive branches as part of peace negotiations. Most of his fellow students couldn't wait to argue, to express their disagreements with such an idea; and an overwhelming class majority concluded our IDF cannot risk cutting back on intelligence gathering, and most thought we must retain and aggressively use our pre-emptive strike capabilities."

"Yes, we must never give up those things!" she agreed. "Israel must always be able to defend itself. Our intelligent network is the best in the world, with Shin Bet, Mossad, Aman, and Lakam. It must stay that way."

"Yes, I know. And I agree we must never—

She was in her nightgown, rinsing her face, wanting to end the discussion and relax her mind before heading for bed. "Surely, dear, someday we'll have a leader who can bring peace."

Nothing more was said until they were in bed. Simon was on his back with his eyes closed, thinking about her last words. *I so hope you're right.* He rolled over and gave her a kiss.

"Good night, honey." She sounded very relaxed. "I'm so thankful you and your students are all safe. Sleep tight."

Chaim was still wide awake, alone in the office of his home, about five miles away. As Mossad's representative on Israel's four men Intelligence Overview Committee, he had spent the past three hours with the police, interrogating people about the university bombing. Ariel Sharon, who most in the intelligence community considered to be the greatest field commander in Israel's history, had also attended the meeting.

Thank goodness Simon wasn't killed. Thoughts of his old friend kept popping in and out of Chaim's mind. He focused on the committee's key conclusions. *We should remove every last Palestinian from the university.* He recalled Sharon's positive reaction to that idea. *He's sharp, and ambitious. He'd be a great Prime Minister; I'd support him if he wants the job.*

On February 6, 2001, Ariel Sharon and his Likud Party won a landslide victory over Ehud Barak for the leadership of Israel. Eight months later, after the Nine-Eleven terrorist attack against the United States, Chaim watched on television as Prime Minister Sharon explained the realities of Arab terrorism to Americans and warned the White House, "Don't try to appease the Arabs at our expense."

Chaim was now a valued member of the Likud Party and an influential person in the Knesset, as well as a senior leader with Mossad. He had spent the entire day in the Knesset, supporting a determination to have Israeli forces drive deeper into Occupied Territories controlled by Palestinians. The top buttons of his shirt were open. He scratched an itch on his neck, then dropped his hands to his lap and began to work his wedding ring in a circle around his pudgy finger. He had married his mistress a week after being elected to the Knesset. The ring still felt strange. He closed his eyes and moved his head from side to side in an effort to ease the tension in his neck.

"Dinner's ready, dear."

Chaim opened his eyes, grabbed the remote, and hit the off button. As he walked to the dining room, he dug his finger into his right nostril to relieve a sudden itch.

"What's on the news?" his wife asked as she put hot plates of food on the table. "I hope the prime minister won't stop until the Hamas and Fatah terrorists are all flat on their backs, dead."

Chaim pulled her chair back from the table. She settled into the chair and he helped her move it closer.

"Dear?" She expected an answer.

Chaim yanked his own chair back. "You're damn right he won't."

Four years later, Chaim was in his office early in the morning, going through mail from the previous day. He opened a small envelope containing a sympathy card in remembrance of his mother, who had passed away at ninety-four. *That was nice of Simon*, Chaim thought as he recalled that Shelley Ha-am had passed away a few years back. Many childhood memories raced through his mind as he looked out the window. The sun was rising, peeking over the top of the concrete Separation Wall far to the east.

We turned things around, he thought. *That wall made a huge difference. And Arafat is gone.* He smiled. *It took us a long time.* He leaned back in the large leather swivel chair, propped his heels on the windowsill, closed his eyes, and tried to remember all the things Ariel Sharon had accomplished over the past few years. *We got out of the Gaza quagmire. We wiped Arafat and his network off the map. We've almost completed the wall. Terrorist activities in the territories are in check.* He smiled. *The Russians are mostly consolidated in the territories. Palestinians are contained in non-contiguous ghettos.* A sense of pride rushed through his veins. *I wonder what Arik'll want to do next. He's talking about establishing a new party, Kadima. If he asks me, I'd tell him we need to destroy Syria, take control in southern Lebanon, and finally establish Israeli control throughout the Levant.* His eyes were still closed as a broad smile swept over his face.

Nine years later

It was January 11, 2014. Simon and his wife were in the den of their West Jerusalem apartment, both intently focused on the chess board. The volume on the television documentary covering the death of Ariel Sharon on January 4 was turned down.

"Checkmate," Simon's wife said as she clapped her hands together and leaned back in her chair.

"Darn!" Simon leaned back and smiled at his wife. "I knew you had me after you made that bishop move. Good strategy." He shifted in his chair and looked at the television.

"Do you think there will ever be peace in our lifetime, dear?"

Simon laughed. "I'm seventy-two and still hopeful. But I wouldn't bet on it. There's probably a better chance we'll experience a major battle, right here in Israel, before we experience a lasting peace."

"I don't follow you."

He thought for a few seconds before answering. "When I think about our leadership and our accomplishments over the past four decades, it's hard for me to explain where we've been trying to go." He paused, tracing through past leaderships in his mind. "Yitzhak Shamir was prime minister, under Likud, when we moved here in early 1988. That's when the Knesset authorized the big push into the Occupied Territories to house immigrants from Russia, and it was really a major change for Israel. We thought, when Labour defeated Likud in mid-1992, Rabin could establish a peace pact; but he was assassinated, and Peres couldn't get Arafat in line before Likud took over again, with Netanyahu." He could see his wife's interest in his summary. "It's been a mess since then. Labour, with Barak in charge, tried for a couple of years; from July 1999 to March 2001. But then Ariel Sharon took over Likud leadership from Netanyahu and kept control until his stroke in April 2006; even after establishing his new Kadima party in 2005. Ehud Olmert took leadership of Kadima after Sharon's stroke, but was defeated by Likud in March 2009, and Netanyahu's been in charge since then."

There was a long silence. Finally, "Who knows what's next?" She reached for the white chess pieces. "I'm glad the boys are back in America with their families. And," she laughed, "I'm ready to skin you in another game."

Two years later

Chaim arrived home mid-afternoon, much earlier than normal. His driver sped away when Chaim started up the front steps. He was limping because of severely stiff knees. Suddenly, the door opened and two ladies dressed in black, with masked faces, stared down at him.

"What the—!" Chaim half-stumbled as he reached for his hidden revolver.

"Hello, Mr. Kahane," said one of the Palestinian cleaning ladies. "We've just finished. Have a nice evening, sir." She and the other lady casually walked past Chaim as he stumbled quickly into the house with his revolver halfway out of the holster.

"What's going on around here?" he loudly demanded.

His wife poked her head around the corner from the kitchen. "Hello, dear. You're home early! What is it?"

"What were they doing here?"

"Those two ladies who just left? They're our cleaning service. They come every second week. You've never met them."

Chaim holstered the revolver and took a deep breath. "I don't want to. Do they ever go into my study?"

"No, dear. I've told you before, I'm the only one that goes into that room. I get them started on the rest of the house and then do your office myself." She paused. "Is something bothering you?"

He opened the closet and took off his jacket. "You're damn right something is bothering me. You must have heard, on the news." He got no reaction. "The Holy See and Vatican finalized an accord with the Palestinians, for operation of the Catholic Church in a Palestinian-controlled part of Jerusalem."

"I heard that," she said without much emotion.

"What the fuck?" Chaim exclaimed. "What's wrong with them? We told them back in June, when they recognized the Palestinian Territories as a sovereign state, that kind of interference is counter-productive to the peace process."

What peace process? She almost snickered aloud as she turned back to her kitchen work and politely offered, "That's too bad."

The two Palestinian cleaning ladies arrived at the Israeli check-stop by bus at about 4:40 p.m. It had been a quiet day for the security guards. The guards recognized the women and nothing was said as they walked through the security gate and continued on the way to their homes in East Jerusalem. They were small in stature, loose-fitting frocks covered their heads, most of their face, their bodies, and their sandals were barely noticeable below their long skirts. Once through the gate, their pace quickened.

"I can hardly wait to hear how the children did at school," one said to the other.

"Me too." She spoke joyfully. "I'm so glad they like their new teacher."

"He seems a good one. Lots of stories for the children about the history of our people. He even tells them stories about a hero who will one day bring all Palestinians back together. It's a fun and encouraging story for the children."

The other nodded. "I like it, too. He gives them hope."

They said nothing for the ten minutes it took to make their way up to the top of the path where, as was their habit, they stopped to catch their breath and look back over the top of the Separation Wall at the rooftops in Israel.

"Maybe someday our grandchildren will live where our grandparents lived."

"Maybe," said the other as they turned to continue the last leg of their journey home. "But really, do you think things will ever change around here?"

They each chuckled at the idea.

STORY 4

EGYPT

CHAPTER 12

LAD FROM CAIRO

May 9, 1964; Cairo, Egypt

Abdel Radwan stood beside the hospital bed looking down at his wife as she nursed their newborn son, Tariq. Abdel was thirty-two years old, a handsome and powerfully built man, tall and muscular. There were slight hints of grey in his pitch-black hair, thick eyebrows, and thinly trimmed moustache. Large dark eyes, an aquiline nose, and thick lips dominated his face.

"The boy looks so strong, my dear." Abdel's eyes sparkled with joy. "Thank you for such a blessing."

She looked small, tucked snugly between huge pillows. Her face lit up with pride. "He will be a fine son, Abdel. And he shall grow to be a fine man, like you, my dear."

Abdel looked at his watch. "My son," he said to his firstborn, "I must go. President Nasser and Premier Khrushchev are waiting for me. I must explain to them how our company is dismantling and moving the Abu Simbel temple for the Aswan Dam project." He kissed his wife, then the baby. As he walked the hospital corridor, his mind turned to the chess game President Nasser had been forced to play with the United States and the USSR. *Our president's walking a tightrope; forced to trust the Soviets because the United States and Britain backed away from their promises to help finance the dam.* He walked down the front steps of the hospital, got into the back seat of the Mercedes, and the car pulled away from the hospital grounds. *If our country could only focus on peace.* He shrugged. *Thanks to Allah, we have the Suez as our ace in the hole.*

The Suez Canal is a 101-mile, sea-level waterway through Egypt connecting the Red and Mediterranean seas. It was first opened in November 1869 by the Universal Suez Ship Canal Company, under French and Egyptian ownership. Owing to debt problems, Egypt was forced to sell its shares in the company to the United Kingdom in 1875. In 1936, Britain was given the right to maintain military forces in the Canal Zone and control entry points, which complemented responsibilities in the British Palestinian Mandate. In 1954, seven years after British forces withdrew from Palestine, British forces also withdrew from the Suez Canal area and left Egypt in control, following which Egypt prohibited the use of the canal by ships destined to and from Israel. In 1956, Egypt nationalized the canal so passage fees could be charged and used to pay for the new Aswan Dam. On October 29, 1956, Israel invaded Egypt with the encouragement of Britain and France, and Egypt completely blocked the canal by intentionally sinking forty ships, creating the Suez Canal Crisis. A truce agreement was developed under the auspices of the United Nations and the canal was reopened in March 1957; however, Israel did not give up the Gaza land it had taken during the invasion and a war of attrition resulted.

Three years later
June 1967

Tariq was barefooted, playing with his toy truck on the tile floor of their large kitchen. His olive-coloured skin contrasted with his white shirt and white pants. His short, straight, pitch-black hair was neatly parted on the right side. When he heard his father come in the front door, his heart danced with joy and he started running, but he stopped in his tracks when he heard his father's angry voice. He crept to the kitchen door and tried to hear what his father was saying.

"How could Nasser have been so naive? Damn!" There was a loud bang and Tariq visualized his father's right fist pounding down hard on the hall table. "He should not have threatened Israel. He should not have told everyone that we would blast the Zionists from existence. Look what they've done to us!"

"It was a grave mistake." Tariq's mother's voice was quiet and soft.

"Our army and air force has been wiped out by Israeli forces," Abdel continued. "They destroyed two hundred of our tanks and more than four hundred of our planes—made mincemeat of our forces. And now they claim control of Jerusalem, an achievement beyond comprehension!"

"What will we do, Abdel?" Tariq sensed his mother's great concern.

Abdel blew his nose and cleared his throat. "Sayyid Qutb was right." He was referring to the brilliant Muslim Brotherhood writer who Nasser had executed by hanging a year earlier. "The Zionists thirst to control everything. They don't want peace." He coughed to clear his throat. "The brotherhood and Nasser must stop fighting each other."

The Muslim Brotherhood was founded as an Islamic fundamentalist organization in 1928 through the initiative of an Egyptian school teacher named al-Banna and a few Suez Canal employees who were intent on promoting renewal of the Islamic ethos. Concern over Zionist control in Palestine and influence in Britain caused the Brotherhood to publish Arab translations of *The Protocols of the Elders of Zion* as a warning. When a military coup overthrew the Farouk monarchy in 1952, the Brotherhood supported but did not share power with the Nasser regime. In 1954, President Nasser abolished the Muslim Brotherhood and imprisoned thousands of its followers. The writer Qutb was released in 1964 and became the Brotherhood's most influential thinker, arguing that Muslim societies in Egypt and other Western-influenced nations were no longer truly Islamic and must be transformed through violent revolution that would overthrow westernized Islamic states. Qutb was arrested again, accused of plotting to overthrow President Nasser's government, put on trial, and hanged in 1966.

Eight months later, four-year-old Tariq sat with his mother and father at the dinner table. He kept rubbing his nose. His mother gave him a threatening look, asking him to stop.

Abdel's attention was elsewhere. His wife stood, took the water jug from the middle of the table, and poured water into her husband's empty glass. "Dear, something is bothering you."

Abdel sipped the water as he waited for her to return to her chair. He placed the glass back on the table. "President Nasser has threatened Israel again."

Tariq looked to his mother and back to his father. He expected his father to explain his concern. Instead, Abdel grabbed his fork and dug it into his food.

"Why does the president make such threats?" his mother asked.

There was an awkward silence while Abdel finished chewing and swallowed. "President Nasser wants to be the leader of the Arab world. He's jealous the Western world is about to acknowledge Arafat as the leader of the PLO. And he has again threatened Israel. That's dangerous."

Tariq had no idea what his father was talking about. He had never heard of the Palestine Liberation Organization, which was founded by the Arab nations in 1964 in hopes of providing a coordinating entity for the nationless Palestinians. He knew only that his father always expressed great disgust and anger whenever Israel was mentioned.

On September 28, 1970, President Nasser died of a heart attack. Abdel Radwan's family mourned the loss. On October 5, Vice-President Anwar Sadat became the new president of Egypt.

"President Sadat will be a great leader of our people," Abdel said to his six-year-old son as they sat on the front steps of their home late in the afternoon.

"What will he do, Father?"

Abdel looked at Tariq. "I think he will bring peace to our world. I think he will work to find a way for the brothers, the Arabs and Jews, to live in peace."

"Arabs and Jews are brothers?" Tariq was confused. "What do you mean?"

Abdel smiled. "We are brothers, Tariq, going back thousands of years."

Tariq looked down and mumbled. "But the Jews call themselves God's chosen people."

Abdel nodded. "Yes, that is true. We are all God's, Allah's, chosen people. We are all brothers in Allah's eyes. That's why our president is such an important man. If President Sadat can convince the Jews to break away from the Zionist terror and join with us in peace, it will be one of the greatest things anyone has ever done for the world."

Tariq had no idea what his father was talking about. "Can President Sadat do that, Father?"

Tariq's mother opened the front door. "Dinner is ready, boys."

Two years later
1972

On September 5, 1972, Tariq was waiting at the door for his father to come home at the end of the workday. "Father, did you hear what happened at the Olympic Games in Germany?"

"Yes, son, I heard. It is an awful tragedy. Eleven Israeli athletes were killed."

"Why? I thought Hamas and Hezbollah only killed Israeli terrorists. The Jewish athletes did nothing. Our teacher says—"

"Come here; sit with me."

Tariq sat in the chair next to his father. Their eyes met.

"Sometimes, Tariq, innocent people pay for the crimes of others. It's a sad day for all good people. A sad day for the cause of Palestine."

"They killed one of my friend's cousins. Why?"

Frustrations. One after the other. Ever since the British bowed to world Zionists. Abdel wanted his son to know the truth. "Remember your history lessons at school, Tariq. Do you remember that the Ottoman Turks once controlled our country?" Tariq nodded. "And then the British defeated the Turks, during the First World War, early this century. Do you remember learning that?"

148

Tariq nodded. "Yes, Father."

"When the Turks controlled things, there was religious peace in the Middle East. Muslims, Christians, and Jews lived side by side in peace. People did what they wanted to do, and without hurting others. The trouble started when the British took over."

Tariq was confused. "Why?"

"That gets too complicated, Tariq. It's too involved for you to try to understand right now." He patted his son's shoulder. "But when you are older we will discuss those details. Maybe by then the Jewish people will have rid themselves—" He coughed. "That's all you need to know right now, son."

One year later
October 6, 1973

The Yom Kippur War started on October 6, 1973. That evening, Tariq greeted his father at the door.

"The radio says we're driving the Zionists into the sea!"

Abdel looked down at his son. He marvelled at how alike they were. "It was a devilish act, son. A bad mistake to attack them during Yom Kippur."

"What's Yom Kippur?"

"It's the most religious of Jewish holidays."

"Like Ramadan?"

Abdel nodded. "Similar."

By October 16, much of Egypt's military had been destroyed and, along with the other attacking Arab nations, the country was seeking a surrender arrangement. It was quiet during dinner. When Tariq's mother started to clear the table, Abdel turned to Tariq.

"No questions tonight, Tariq?"

Tariq's eyes were down. He worked the muscles of his nose in an effort to ease the itch. He shook his head.

"The United Nations called for a ceasefire today," Abdel offered. "But Israel's Prime Minister, Golda Meir, refuses to abide. Do you know why?"

"Why?" Tariq grumbled.

"She says we're not yet beaten enough!" Abdel's eyes bore into Tariq. "There's a lesson in this."

Tariq looked up. "What?"

Abdel's stare became more intense. "Never start a physical fight, Tariq, not unless you know, for sure and without question, you can win it. And, once you start, make sure you win it. Quickly!" The last word was loaded with anger as Abdel stood, turned from the table, threw his powerful shoulders back, and walked toward his study. *We would have won this war if the Americans had stayed out of it. Zionists have greater influence in Washington than we ever imagined.* He forced a smile. *The oil embargo will teach the Americans!*

Six years later
March 26, 1979

Tariq was fifteen years old and well educated. He was at the top of his class in science and mathematics, but it was history, economics, and modern politics that stirred his emotions more than anything else.

"Tariq, what do you think of U.S. President Carter getting President Sadat and Prime Minister Begin to sign a peace agreement today?"

"It's wonderful, Father. Just like you told me long ago, President Sadat will bring peace. I now respect America because of what President Carter helped to accomplish."

"I hope you're right, son. Time will tell."

On March 31, the foreign ministers of eighteen Arab and Islamic nations met in Baghdad to condemn President Sadat's agreement with Israel. They cut off diplomatic and economic relations with Egypt and those actions were endorsed by the Palestine Liberation Organization.

"Why is everyone against the peace agreement?" This was Tariq's first question when Abdel arrived at the breakfast table. "Why are they condemning President Sadat?"

"They think the president signed an agreement with the Devil." Abdel settled into his chair. "They believe there can never be peace as long as Zionists control Jerusalem and the Occupied Territories."

"What will happen?"

"We'll have to wait and see. I have a lot of things on my mind, son. We'll talk more this evening."

In July 1979, Israel withdrew from parts of the Sinai. In September, Israel shot down Syrian fighter planes over Lebanon. On November 4, Iranian students seized control of the U.S. Embassy building in Tehran. In December, Soviet Russia was moving troops into Afghanistan. The Middle East was beginning to boil over.

In early 1980, Islamic nations demanded that the Soviet Union withdraw troops from Afghanistan. Tariq and his father met in the dining room. Tariq, now sixteen, was a couple of inches shorter than Abdel but his shoulders seemed as broad and almost as powerful.

"I don't really understand why the Soviets want to control Afghanistan?"

Abdel shrugged. "The Mujahedeen are causing troubles for the Soviets. The United States is supporting the Mujahedeen. It's becoming another part of the Cold War."

Tariq was puzzled. "Why would America support Islamic people in Afghanistan? They're against Muslims here, and in Palestine, and in Lebanon. Everywhere else."

His father chuckled. "That's a good question. America is a confused nation. It is too powerful and can be a great danger to the world as long as Washington is strongly influenced by—"

"I don't understand," Tariq interrupted.

"You'll understand someday."

In April 1981, Israeli jets shot down two Syrian helicopters over Lebanon and the Israeli military shelled a beach in Lebanon, killing and wounding many. On June 7, an Israeli air raid destroyed an atomic reactor in Iraq. Later in the month, Moshe Dayan declared Israel was capable of making nuclear bombs.

"We've known that for some time," Abdel said when his wife brought up the subject at dinner. "I'm surprised Moshe Dayan admitted it."

"Are they trying to frighten us?" Tariq asked.

"Maybe, but we already knew."

It was fall, 1981. Tariq, seventeen years old, arrived home after a day of work with his father's construction company. He sported a small moustache, wore tan pants, and his open shirt exposed his powerful chest. He spotted the envelope on the table in the front hallway with the Harvard University logo in the top left-hand corner. The letter said he was accepted into Harvard Engineering College. Later that evening, Tariq and his father sat in the den discussing the events of the day and the discussion, as so often happened, turned to Israel.

"I'm concerned, Tariq." Abdel's worry was etched on his face. "The Zionists are getting more militant, much more aggressive. They're pushing Jewish settlements deeper and deeper into the Occupied Territories and driving thousands more Palestinians from their homes every month."

"Why doesn't the United Nations do something to stop it?" Tariq reacted. "It's been going in the wrong direction since President Sadat was assassinated by one of our own soldiers on October 6. President Mubarak doesn't seem as strong and presidential, nor as internationally respected as was Anwar Sadat."

Abdel shrugged. "Much depends on the United States. If the U.S. energy crisis continues, they'll probably put some pressure on Israel."

"Do you think Egypt's in danger again? Perhaps I shouldn't go to Harvard."

Abdel did not react immediately. He was thinking about changes he had been sensing in business dealings during the past several months. "One day, you will be responsible for running our company, Tariq. I'm sensing changes occurring in the business ethics of Americans, and we will always need to adjust to the ways of that great nation." He looked into his son's eyes. "You go to Harvard, son. You try to understand Americans and the Christian people of the West. Someday, your wisdom will be required. You go to Harvard. Learn all you can, and do your very best."

CHAPTER 13

DEEPER IN TROUBLE

Six years later
1988

Tariq completed his studies at Harvard in 1987. Abdel gave him more and more responsibility in the growing construction company. Much of Tariq's time was spent travelling to countries throughout the Middle East. It was mid-week and they were at their desks at the company office in Cairo, backs to each other as they talked and studied papers at the same time.

"We should not bid on that project." It was an order, not an opinion. "I don't trust Saddam." Abdel shifted a paper into his out-basket. "Involvement could rebound against us."

Tariq swivelled his chair around to face his father's back. "I understand, but there's no proof they're doing anything other than replacing the nuclear plant Israel destroyed seven years ago. If the Iraqis ask us to—"

Abdel had swivelled his chair to face Tariq and held up his hand for silence. "Ever since President Sadat's assassination, Saddam has dreamed of becoming leader of the whole Arab world. He does not want peace with Israel under any conditions. I don't trust him."

Tariq was determined to bid on the project. "The Zionists don't want peace either. Everywhere I go there's concern about how they've gained such influence and power."

"Tariq, we can support all other Iraqi activities, but not the reconstruction of that nuclear plant. It's too sensitive." Abdel stood and starting walking away. "I need to relieve myself. That's all I want to hear on the subject."

In December 1990, the United Nations General Assembly called for the convening of an international peace conference on the Middle East, and reaffirmed its conviction that the core of the bothersome conflict with Iraq was the question of Palestine. On December 20, the UN Security Council requested the secretary-general to make new efforts to monitor and observe the situation of Palestinian civilians, and urged Israel to apply the terms of the 1949 Geneva Convention relative to the protection of civilians. Israel rejected the UN proposal. A month later, the UN secretary-general urged Saddam Hussein to comply with Security Council resolutions and withdraw from Kuwait.

Two years later

Tariq and his father were sitting in the study of the family home after dinner. They had been discussing the Oslo Peace Agreement. Tariq looked happy. His father was deep in thought.

"Why do you think I am too optimistic?" Tariq asked.

Abdel did not answer immediately. His mind was on what happened after President Sadat and Prime Minister Begin signed the Camp David Peace Accord many years earlier. *That agreement just angered the extremists.* "I hope this agreement has a better destiny than the one in 1979," he finally answered.

"President Sadat never had the support of the Arab nations in 1979," Tariq argued. "This time the agreement's between Arafat and Rabin."

Abdel nodded. "I know, but I don't trust either of them. Arafat can't control Hamas or his Fatah terrorists. And I honestly believe the Zionists will never agree to give up an inch of the land they've already stolen." He paused. "Since Clinton defeated President Bush in the last U.S. election, the Zionists have been getting more and more aggressive." He shrugged. "I don't know. If this agreement succeeds in bringing permanent peace, I'll be surprised."

Five years later
Late 1998

Tariq and his father were at the office late one evening. They had been discussing new business prospects for the company. Tariq drank the last of his soda water and started to get up from his chair.

"We need to discuss something else."

Tariq settled back into the chair. "What's on your mind?"

Abdel yawned. "Too many things are getting out of hand." He shook his head. "Hamas and Fatah are building for war because Israeli forces are tearing Palestine apart again. Saddam is making threatening noises. Rumours are rampant about bin Laden broadening his al-Qaeda network. And there's something else." He paused. "Have you ever heard the term Arab Spring?"

Tariq nodded. "A few times. Think it's just another enlightenment thing."

"I don't know." Abdel sounded puzzled. "It might go beyond that. When I was in the hospital for my checkup last week, there was a man in the bed next to me. A very religious man. Anyway, he was under a lot of drugs and kept mumbling about civil wars and asking Allah to turn things into an Arab Spring." Abdel shook his head.

Two years later
2000

By 2000, Tariq was the driving force behind the family's thriving construction business. He was thirty-six years old and the spitting image of his father at the same age. Abdel had experienced some serious health problems and it was noticeable in his appearance; his hair was completely grey, his eyes looked clouded, his shoulders were slumped, and his movements were slow. They were together at the office on August 21.

"The meeting President Mubarak had with President Clinton yesterday was really discouraging," Abdel said. "I still can't believe Clinton left the meeting with a warning that Middle East peace might not be possible. I don't think he would have said that if he thought Barak could win re-election in Israel."

"I know," Tariq reacted. "There's a lot of unrest, a sense of helplessness, everywhere I go. No one is optimistic about Middle East peace."

On October 12, a bomb blew a gaping hole in the hull of the *USS Cole* while it was in harbour off the coast of Yemen. And, during the following months, Egypt and most of the world watched on television as Israeli tanks and helicopters focused on destroying Yasser Arafat's compound in Ramallah and several other Palestinian towns as the vicious cycle of terrorism/counter-terrorism between Israelis and Palestinians intensified.

Tariq sensed there was some hope when the United Nations finally condemned Israel for the disproportionate nature of its violence against the Palestinian leadership and innocent civilians. *The UN should send in peacekeeping forces and place blockades or sanctions on Israel,* he thought. *No other nation could get away with this continuing brutality. Something has to give!*

A year later
September 11, 2001; Cairo

It was 9:15 in the evening and Tariq was still busy at the office when the telephone rang. He picked up the receiver. "Hello?"

"Tariq," his father's voice cracked with panic, "are you watching television?"

"No, wha—"

"Put it on, right now, to CNN."

Tariq grabbed the remote and clicked the button. "What is it?"

"Have you got CNN on?"

"Yes!" Tariq felt a strange panic. "What's—?"

"It's the World Trade Center in Manhattan, Tariq. Two airplanes loaded with passengers were flown into the top floors of the two towers and they both crumbled to the ground. It's a disaster! I'll call you back in an hour or so. We need to determine what really happened. It may be a Zionist trick, or it could be another incident like the *Cole*."

"I'll make a few calls to see what I can find out."

An hour later, the office door opened and Abdel limped in. "I couldn't just sit at home and watch that disaster. What have you heard?"

"Nothing. Everyone I've talked to is bewildered and frightened. Frightened that the Americans will blame—"

"It's unbelievable! Al Qaeda again, or a Zionist plot, or a fundamentalist Christian plot. Unbelievable!" Abdel slumped into his chair.

Nations around the world had no idea what would happen next. On October 10, Tariq sat as an observer during a meeting of the League of Arab Nations in Doha, Qatar. Senior representatives from all Arab nations were seated around the large conference table. Some were yelling and shouting. Others were cautious about what they said. Things finally settled down and concerns began to be rationally expressed.

After the meeting, Tariq summarized things in his mind. *Everyone's concerned and frightened. No idea what the Americans will do next. They're already bombing Afghanistan because Taliban rulers won't hand bin Laden over to them. Some expect the Zionists are pressuring the White House to blame Saddam and pushing to put American troops on the ground in Iraq. Some want to sanction oil shipments to Britain and the United States to limit their military campaigns.* He breathed deeply in an effort to relieve tension.

CHAPTER 14

DISTANT LOVE

Three years later
May 2004; Cairo

Tariq spent the morning in meetings at the company's main office in Old Cairo's business district not far from the Mogamma Central Government buildings. At noon, he drove his Benz W140 east to the Al Muski section for lunch on the patio of Studio Masr. The day was relatively clear, and many of Cairo's landmarks were prominent in the distance. *The city's spectacular on clear days*, he thought as he flipped his cell phone on. Several texts needing immediate response. After a lunch of Greek salad and bread, he left Studio Masr and took the Salah Salem freeway to the Fairmont Heliopolis Cairo Hotel near the Cairo International Airport. *We did a good job with this hotel*, he thought proudly as he recalled some of the difficulties encountered during construction. It was 2:55 p.m. when he stopped in front of the hotel.

The valet opened his car door. "Welcome, Mr. Radwan. Nice to see you. They're expecting you in Room 450."

"Thank you." Tariq left the car running and headed into the hotel.

The door of Suite 450 was open. Carol Fulton was sitting at a table with her cameraman. One of the leading anchor announcers for TST Television Network, Ms. Fulton was meeting with people in the Middle East as part of a documentary film on the status of the U.S. invasion and occupation of Iraq. She looked up. "Hello. Mr. Radwan?"

Tariq nodded and smiled. *She's as fresh and beautiful as she looks on TV*, he thought.

"Come in," Ms. Fulton stood. "We're summarizing our day so far." She was wearing a light-blue blouse and navy skirt and her dark-brown eyes were alive with welcome.

Tariq towered over the lady. He held out his hand. "I'm very pleased to meet you, Ms. Fulton."

"Please, call me Carol." They shook hands and she motioned to her left. "Eric's my cameraman." Her attention shifted appropriately. "Mr. Radwan."

Tariq and Eric nodded their greetings. "Hello, Eric. Pleased to meet you. Please, call me Tariq." They shook hands.

Carol fitted a small microphone to the lapel of Tariq's jacket. As they settled into comfortable armchairs facing the camera, she explained the interview would be taped, not live. There was a small table between them with bottles of water. Eric started the camera. Carol looked into the camera and explained Tariq was an Egyptian construction contractor with business contacts throughout the Middle East, then turned to him. "Mr. Radwan, I'm sure you know many government and business leaders throughout the Middle East."

Tariq nodded. "Yes, I do."

"Do you think most Middle East nations are pleased with having Saddam Hussein removed from power in Iraq?"

"I don't think I'd put it that way."

She waited, hoping Tariq would elaborate, but he didn't. It was an awkward pause. "Most people I've spoken to so far seem to be relieved that Saddam is no longer in power."

"I suppose that's true, in some cases."

This isn't going to be an easy interview, she thought. "Saddam's weapons of—"

"There were no weapons," Tariq interrupted as he casually reached for his bottle of water, removed the cap, and took a drink.

"What do you think should be done in Iraq now, Mr. Radwan?"

Tariq placed the bottle back on the table and took a few seconds before answering. "Somehow—" Tariq shrugged slightly in a gesture of hopelessness, "peace and effective government must be restored before things get totally out of hand."

"What do you think could be done?"

"Well, it's become quite a quagmire. I'm not sure. We certainly don't want it to become another Palestine."

Carol was taken aback by the reference. "Would you care to be more specific?"

Tariq rubbed his nose and his forefinger passed over his closely trimmed moustache. He cleared his throat. "We don't want the U.S. military to do in Iraq what the Zionist military did," his pause was unnaturally long, "is still doing in Palestine."

Finally, Carol thought, *we've hit a nerve*. "You don't seriously believe the circumstances are similar?" It was a question. "Most Americans are devastated with what's happening to both the Palestinian and Iraqi people. You must know. It's not the American way to—"

"Oh?" Tariq interrupted. He paused only briefly. "I watched Henry Kissinger and Madeleine Albright making much the same claim on CNN the other day." He cleared his throat and looked into Carol's eyes. "We believe what we see, not what we hear."

"What do you think should be done in Iraq?" she repeated.

Tariq shrugged. "How should I know? I expect the U.S. needs to find a way to get out of there and most other parts of the Middle East without leaving the places in a state of civil war."

"Do you think the UN should be involved?"

"Of course, but not in the wishy-washy way it has handled Palestine for so many—"

"Do you think the UN could handle such a task?"

"Of course it could, with proper U.S. support. The problem is not with the UN, it's with America."

"How is that?"

"It's a long story."

I can't waste any more time with him, she thought. "Unfortunately, we haven't time for that, Mr. Radwan. Thank you so much for giving us your outlook on the situation." She turned and looked into the camera. "This is TST. You have just witnessed another exclusive interview in our effort to uncover the simple truth." She breathed a sigh of relief and started to remove the microphone from her blouse as Eric turned the camera off.

Tariq had been enjoying the dialog and it took him a few seconds to realize they were finished. He took another drink of water, removed the microphone from his lapel, and stood as he handed it to Carol. There was no eye contact. "Could I ask you to dinner this evening, Ms. Fulton?"

Carol pressed her lips together in an effort to control her complete surprise and anger. *He's got balls!* But something made her pause before answering. She took a deep breath, looked up with challenge in her eyes, and forced a smile. "You could, Mr. Radwan and—" a slight change of tone to indicate she was still the one in control of the meeting, "I accept." She turned away and started talking to Eric.

At 8:00 that evening, Tariq was waiting at the entrance to the dining room at the top of the Fairmont Heliopolis Hotel. He was casually dressed in dark slacks, a light-brown sports jacket, and patterned sport-shirt open at the collar, and was about to check his watch when Carol walked out of the elevator.

She's beautiful, he thought as she walked toward him and held out her hand. She was wearing a full-length black and white evening dress, and her wavy red-brown hair fell almost to her shoulders. As he took her small hand in his and looked down into brown eyes dancing with energy, Tariq sensed how his father must have felt in the company of his mother.

During dinner, Tariq discovered Carol had grown up in western Canada. *She's got a good grasp of the world oil industry*, he concluded rather quickly. They were almost finished the main course when the waiter opened the second bottle of red wine and poured some into a clean glass for Tariq to sample. He nodded approval and the waiter turned to Carol.

She held her hand over the glass. "I'm fine. No more, thank you."

Music started to play as the waiter filled Tariq's glass. "Do you dance?" Tariq asked.

"Sometimes." Under the table, her feet were already moving to the music.

Tariq smiled. "Well, this group is quite good. It's from Canada." He grinned at her look of surprise. "If you like to dance maybe—" He stopped when she looked at the waiter and nodded.

They danced for the next two hours. With each dance, Tariq sensed she wanted him to hold her closer.

"What a wonderful time," Carol said as they left the dining room. "I haven't had so much fun in a long time."

"Me either," Tariq agreed as he pressed the elevator button. "When do you go back to New York?" He turned and looked into her eyes.

"I have another day of interviews."

"You leave tomorrow evening?"

"No, the next morning."

Tariq smiled. "Have you plans for tomorrow evening?"

She smiled back. "I thought you'd never ask."

The next evening, they dined while cruising on the River Nile. Tariq pointed out many of the landmarks of Cairo and told stories about ancient and modern Egypt. After dinner, they walked the deck. For a while, they discussed the world oil industry.

"High oil prices are damaging the U.S. economy," Carol opined.

Tariq was looking out at the water. "Maybe Washington should reduce the tariffs and sales taxes it collects on Middle East oil."

Carol laughed. "I expect they've never thought about that." She stopped walking and turned to look up at him. "But, Tariq, how high do you think oil prices can go before the world economy collapses?"

He shrugged. "A long way, I expect. Right now, Americans pay more for a bottle of water and hundreds of times more for a good bottle of wine than they pay for an equivalent volume of gasoline." He smiled. "There's a long way to go."

"Really?" It was clear Carol wanted him to explain.

"It's important to realize that the primary focus of our Middle East oil has already shifted to Asia and Eastern markets. The West is still important, but the Asian economies are booming; they're investing lots of capital in the Middle East, and their labour costs and taxes are low. Those countries could withstand a significant increase in oil prices and still have their products compete in the world markets."

They were strolling casually. "How much of an increase?" Carol asked.

"I've heard talk that sixty dollars a barrel would not be unreasonable."

"Impossible!" She stopped abruptly. They were standing near the railing. She grabbed it and looked up at the black sky and dripping stars. "That would be a disaster!"

"It would be about the same price as a barrel of soda pop." Tariq laughed as he placed his arm around her back.

She managed to laugh, and looked up into his eyes. "This has been so special. Thank you."

"It's been special for me, too." Tariq gave her a tender squeeze. "You're a special lady." He released her and they resumed the walk.

"How can we feel such peace and pleasure when the world seems to be falling apart?" she asked.

"This, like we are right now, is how it should be," Tariq said. "The rest of it, the problems created by bankers and politicians and religious fanatics and fundamentalists, it will eventually pass. It has to, even if it takes another great war."

There was concern in her eyes when she turned and looked up. Tariq turned to face her, gently placed his powerful hands on her shoulders, looked into her eyes, and their lips touched.

Ten years later
March 2014; Sydney, Australia

It was 7:30 a.m. when Tariq and Carol walked out of the ocean-side villa and down the steps to the dock. Carol was wearing a light-yellow blouse, shorts, and thongs on her bare feet. The bright sun brought out the rust-red streaks in her brown wavy hair. Tariq wore a light-blue, short-sleeved shirt, shorts, and thongs. His hair was short and he had no moustache.

Since their meeting in Cairo in the spring of 2004, they had maintained a close friendship and love affair. Both were in their late forties and still primarily focused on their respective business responsibilities halfway across the world from each other. Each year, they had managed to meet for two weeks at a secluded and low-profile paradise location—Brazil, Peru, New Zealand, various Australian coastal locations, the coast of Taiwan, Russia, and last year in Switzerland.

Two bellmen followed them with their luggage. The captain of the schooner greeted them and embraced Tariq as an old friend before motioning them aboard. Two burly crew members took the luggage from the bellmen. The five of them were the only ones on the schooner.

It was nearing the end of summer in Australia, the sun was warm, and it wasn't long before Carol had her bathing suit on and her legs dangling over the edge of the schooner as it made its way through the inlet to open ocean waters. They lunched on deck while the schooner headed along the coast. As usual, their conversation soon got around to discussing current world affairs. They had purposely stayed clear of touchy subjects until the plates were cleared from the table.

"How do you think Obama's doing so far in his second term?" Tariq asked.

"I think he's focused," Carol answered without hesitation. "I hope he slows down the bankers' rush to embrace globalism. My dad claims globalization of our markets has turned Canada's development back a hundred years. I hope the president will push to break up major corporations too big to fail; that fiasco in 2008 has ruined our economies."

Tariq stood. "That was a good lunch. I'm going back to dangle my feet over the edge."

A few minutes later they were sitting side by side on the edge of the deck. The boat was moving slowly and the sea was calm.

"A penny for your thoughts," he offered.

"I'm not sure where to start."

"No rush. I'm enjoying this sea breeze."

"Things always seem to be changing in the Middle East," she finally said. "The Muslim Brotherhood's been in and out of charge in your country, and the Arab Spring stuff seems be spreading. Why can't things stabilize? The Sufis, Sunnis, and Shia are always battling. Why can't Islamic nations find a way to establish peace throughout the Middle East?"

He looked at her and chuckled. "Things have never been stable in the Middle East during my lifetime." He paused as different thoughts raced through his mind. "It's impossible to have stability when the Western nations are constantly trying to control our economies, encourage the spread of powerful weaponry all over the place, use their unlimited paper money in exchange for whatever valued commodities they want, and continuously use their worldwide media networks to sped lies and falsehoods."

She turned to him. "Our economies are free, Tariq. Yours are always—"

Tariq stared at her in disbelief. "Free!?" He took a deep breath. "Your people and governments are puppets for those who use that abstraction."

"What?"

He looked into her eyes. "You're too smart not to know what I'm saying. People in the West just won't admit what's really happening. That's not freedom."

"But—"

Tariq's mind was racing with thoughts he had never expressed. "You Westerners think you know all about Shias and Sunnis, about Sufis, about Arabs, about the conflicts you've created in the Middle East. But I ask you, what do you really know about the people who have control over your own economies?" He laughed. "Americans are free all right! Free to make noise, even jokes about everybody else, especially others who are trying to maintain life in the face of great hardships, even terror. Those situations are often great tragedies for those living inside them. The world is tired of the great lattice of wars that won't end." The sudden silence was deafening.

"Wow! I'm sorry I asked!" Carol forced a soft laugh. "I've never sensed such anger in you, Tariq, not since our first interview in the hotel years ago." A more lighthearted chuckle. "Bet you can't repeat what you just said!"

"Sorry, I got carried away." He waved his legs in the breeze. "But, really, it's time Westerners realized the truth about their so-called freedom. You're at the mercy of a hidden empire. If it wanted to break America into battling pockets of individual, self-centred states, I expect it could do that in a heartbeat."

"Hidden empire?"

"Forget it. I got too— forget it."

A soft breeze played with their bare legs and feet. The silence was peaceful, but Carol's mind was swirling.

"No, Tariq," she turned to him, "I won't forget it!" She laughed. "I'm a reporter, and I'm after any troublemaking information I can get." Another chuckle. "What's this all about; a hidden empire that's got control of America?"

Tariq smiled. "Honey, we've been dealing with the same, not so deeply hidden, empire in the Middle East for almost a century. It controls the money of the world, and it has taken a stronger and stronger stranglehold on American politics over the past several decades. It hides in the shadows. I don't know all the details, but I know it exists." He swivelled around and wrapped her in his arms. "Maybe that's your task, to bring it all out in the open."

They kissed.

STORY 5

CANADA

CHAPTER 15

CANADIAN SWEETHEART

Thirty-two years earlier
Spring 1982; Calgary, Alberta, Canada

Her feet floated magically, twisting, tapping, in and out, up and down, spinning, as if they would never stop and her arms moved gracefully in seemingly haphazard directions, all somehow in perfect rhythm. Her long, soft-blue graduation dress with small ruffles at the shoulders and around the bottom clung to her five-foot-six athletic body and swirled loosely just above her ankles. Her breasts and shoulders displayed both femininity and athleticism. Long, wavy, red-brown hair framed her face, brushing against one cheek and then the other, swinging as if in slow motion with the momentum of her dance. When the music stopped, the bandleader announced a fifteen-minute intermission.

Carol Fulton used both hands to brush her hair back from her face, exposing her narrow rosy cheeks and high cheekbones. Thick waves of hair settled softly to her shoulders. Several male wallflowers seemed in a trance as they watched Carol walk off the dance floor with her partner, toward them. She was breathing heavily. Her teeth glistened, her lips seemed so inviting, and her dark-brown

175

eyes danced with laugher in reaction to something her partner was saying.

"Hey, Carol," offered the quarterback of the high school football team, "you've got it going tonight!"

She laughed. "You haven't seen anything yet." She looked him in the eye. "How about you and me, right after intermission?"

"Jeez, you'd wear me out!" He was serious.

"Chicken!"

They all laughed and continued chatting as they ordered soft drinks. A few minutes later, one of her girlfriends asked, "What're you doing this summer, Carol?"

"My Uncle Charlie wants me to work at his radio station. I think it's to do with research into the oil industry."

"Wow. That sounds important. You'll probably make lots of money."

Carol smiled. "I'm lucky, that's for sure."

She was valedictorian of the graduating class. It was well known that she excelled in mathematics and the sciences, but few realized her real love was history and people. She was looking forward to taking an arts degree at university, majoring in communications and media.

For years, Alberta had been the heartland of Canada's petroleum industry. Oil prices and Canadian energy exports to the United States were still at an all-time high due to the Oil Weapon imposed by Arab nations in October 1973.

"Change is in the wind," her Uncle Charlie explained while they sat together her first day on the job. "Western Canada's economy might be heading into another serious slowdown, especially in Alberta. This radio station needs to accurately understand and report what and why things happen as they do. The research I'd like you to do, Carol, will be an important part of that understanding." His smile indicated his confidence. "Your dad has worked in the oil industry for years, so I think that would be the best place for you to start." He pushed a folder across the desk. "There's a list of other industry leaders in here who probably have some clear and definite opinions. I expect they'll gladly speak with you, if you give them a call."

That Sunday evening, after Carol and her mother had washed the dishes and cleaned up the kitchen, she went into the den and sat down with her father.

He turned the TV off. "So, honey, what did you want to talk about?"

"Uncle Charlie wants me to develop a background on the status of Alberta's oil industry. I'll be interviewing a few people; but, Dad, can you maybe get me started?"

He smiled. "I'll do my best. Get something to write on, because I'll probably ramble all over the place."

While Carol went for a pen and pad of paper, her father took his mug to the kitchen and half-filled it with coffee. He was ready when she returned.

"I think it's best to go back to when the oil industry got seriously started in Alberta, which was not all that long ago. It was after the Second World War. Up to that time the United States had been the largest oil-producing nation in the world. But by the late 1940s, most of those U.S. oilfields were depleting and the major oil companies—Jersey Standard, Chevron, Texaco, Mobil and others—were exploring for giant reserves in places such as Venezuela, the Middle East, and in Canada.

"You've heard a lot of my stories about working on the Imperial rig that discovered oil in Leduc in 1947. That was exciting. I had quit high school to go to war, and when I returned, I wanted to make money working on the rigs. A year after the Leduc discovery, your grandma and grandpa convinced me to finish high school, and after that I went into the petroleum engineering program at Oklahoma University; because, by that time, it was pretty clear that Alberta was becoming the centre of the next oil rush in North America.

"I worked the summers with Imperial, and permanently joined Texaco's production department when I graduated in 1954." He laughed. "I can't believe that was almost thirty years ago! I was twenty-seven at the time. A lot of war veterans older than me took a similar route. It was five years of bachelorhood in the oilfields before I found your mother in Moose Jaw. You came along four years after we were married. Our greatest blessing ever!"

"Thanks, Dad." Carol had heard the same story more than once before. "And now you're responsible for the management of all those Alberta oil and gas fields. Saskatchewan, too."

"I'm fortunate, honey. I depend upon many good people to keep things going. But the politicians—" He stopped himself. "I shouldn't get ahead of myself."

He finished his coffee and put the empty mug on the table.

"After the 1947 Leduc discovery, quite a few oilfields were discovered and we needed to get the oil to large refineries in the United States and eastern Canada. Imperial Oil initiated the idea of the Interprovincial Pipeline system from Edmonton to refineries in the U.S. Midwest, Sarnia, and Toronto. Prime Minister St. Laurent and his federal Liberal government authorized the building of the system, as well as the Trans Mountain Pipeline System from

Edmonton to Vancouver and Seattle. Both those pipelines were operational by the late 1950s. It opened vast markets for western Canadian oil. I think it was about 1957 that John Diefenbaker and his Conservative government created a Canadian National Energy Program to protect all Canadian markets west of the Ottawa Valley for western oil producers."

Carol had been busily taking notes. "Protect? What do you mean?"

Her father took a deep breath.

"Well, until we developed our Alberta oil fields and constructed those pipelines, the large refineries in Quebec and Ontario had used imported oil, most of it from Venezuela. Diefenbaker's energy program protected the large Ontario market, with its refineries in Sarnia and Toronto areas, for western producers who shipped through the Interprovincial Pipeline system."

"And the Quebec markets?"

He shook his head. "Quebec has always insisted on paying the lowest price possible for its crude oil. It has never agreed to support western oil development. Only after the 1973 Yom Kippur War did Quebec holler and scream to get our western crude at prices controlled by the federal government." He grabbed his empty mug. "I think I'll get a beer."

Carol made some notes while her father went to the kitchen.

"The energy crisis changed a lot of things here in Calgary, didn't it?" Carol said when he returned with his beer and sat down. "You worked so hard on that Arctic Gas Project. I remember how Calgary seemed to double in size over night."

"I was just thinking about the battles between Premier Lougheed and Prime Minister Trudeau." He took a swig and put his beer mug on the table. "Our federal government has always been controlled

179

by Ontario and Quebec, and those provinces were determined to control Alberta's oil exports, establish guaranteed oil prices for their provincial refineries, and ensure any windfall profits were captured by Ottawa." His mind was back in the mid-1970s. "Trudeau's government created the Foreign Investment Review Act in 1974, and Petro-Canada was established as a federally owned and fully integrated oil and gas crown corporation a year later.

"Trudeau even had Petro-Canada Square built as the tallest building in Calgary, just to show Calgary and all Albertans who was boss!" He forced a chuckle. "The western media called it Red Square, but most of us called it—" he hesitated to use the term.

"What?"

He laughed as he grabbed his mug and held it high. "We called it Trudeau's Erection!"

Carol let out a boisterous laugh. "Father!"

"No kidding! That's what we all called it."

He took another swig.

"Anyway, things just got worse and worse. The end result of it all is that Ottawa's National Energy Board destroyed the opportunity for major pipeline developments through the Mackenzie Valley corridor, and Trudeau's NEP changed the whole fabric of our energy industry. Ottawa introduced new tax and grant systems to discourage foreign investment and encourage the involvement of eastern Canadians; most of whom were only interested in money, and had no idea how to explore for and operate oil and natural gas companies. It made a great mess of our industry at the expense of Canadian taxpayers, especially westerners. Some say our Alberta economy has lost about $100 billion in revenues already. And the revenue sharing agreement that Lougheed finally signed with Trudeau last year won't really—"

"Did Premier Lougheed have any choice?" Carol interrupted.

"Some influential people wanted the West to separate from Canada, maybe even join forces with western U.S. states, but that's a huge step. And really, Premier Lougheed had no choice." He paused briefly. "It was an opportunity taken away from us, and there may never be another chance. The energy crisis is all but over now. Politicians in Ottawa prevented us from taking advantage of a seven-year window of opportunity to establish a powerful oil and natural gas supply network for North America.

"Others are now filling the U.S. energy gap, and we'll be standing on the sidelines as swing suppliers for a long time to come. Oil and gas prices are sure to level out or even decline, our Canadian market will probably shrink as Quebec and the rest of eastern Canada again decide to import cheaper crude from the Middle East, and I'm betting our planned heavy oil developments could even be put on hold. We missed the boat because of the eastern power grab. Or our own stupidity. Or both. Alberta could be looking at a recession within the year!"

"Really?"

"Don't worry, honey. It's a good time for you to be going to university. And Uncle Charlie has given you a perfect summer job."

A few weeks later, Carol and her father were again sitting together in the den one evening. Carol was reading through a draft of her weekly report to Uncle Charlie. Her father was watching the CBC news on television while sipping from a glass of scotch on ice. When the news stopped for commercial, Carol put her report on her lap and looked at her father.

"Need to ask you something, Dad."

"What is it?"

"In all the interviews I've had, everyone is angry at Ottawa. Even Americans, who came here to work, think Ottawa has raped Alberta of its heritage. Some Canadian executives talk as if they wish Alberta and the other western provinces would create a new nation here in the west. They say it would create better understandings and trade agreements for us." She paused. "Can you explain the politics of the whole thing to me?"

He put his glass down. "We touched on a few of those things a couple of weeks ago." He cleared his throat. "Albertans will always be angry about the whole thing. I'm sure we didn't discuss how the Conservatives managed to defeat Trudeau in 1979. I think the reality was that the Liberals defeated themselves when they agreed to let one of the wealthiest individuals in Quebec leave the country without paying the billions of dollars he owed in federal taxes. If the Conservative leader who replaced Trudeau as Prime Minister—" he paused. "You've met Joe Clark, he's an Albertan. If he had been a bit savvier as a politician, he might have lasted long enough to do something good for the West. As it turned out, Trudeau got back into power and strangled us with his National Energy Program."

"Do you think I should include any of that stuff in a report for Uncle Charlie?"

"No, don't do that. It gets too involved and argumentative. Just report on the energy crisis and the part Albertans and western Canadians tried to play. That's all you can say from where you sit."

He paused.

"Western Canadians learned some tough lessons over the past ten years, honey." He shrugged. "But I think it's too late for those lessons to do us any good!"

A month later, Carol was sitting in Uncle Charlie's office. "You've done a fine job this summer, Carol." He had her latest report on his desk. "You've got the makings of a fine reporter."

Carol smiled. "Thanks."

Nine years later
February 1991; Calgary, Alberta

"Ladies and gentlemen, this is your captain. We're starting our descent to the Calgary International Airport and will be on the ground in approximately fifteen minutes. Please keep your seat belts fastened."

Carol stopped reading, checked her seat-belt, and looked out the window of the Air Canada DC-10. There were light clouds in the west. She could see the City of High River. *We're about thirty miles south of mid-town Calgary.*

It was almost 5:30 p.m. To the west, she could see the snow-capped Rocky Mountains framed by a red sunset. She had been home only once since going to work for TST Television Network in New York City, following the 1988 Calgary Winter Olympics about three years ago. TST was a relatively new and small television network; its initials stood for The Simple Truth. Carol's responsibilities related to the world energy industry, and she had already produced some provocative documentaries.

Her latest report pointed out, "World oil prices during the past eighteen years have ranged from $21 per barrel just before the Yom

Kippur War in 1973 to a peak of over $109 in 1980. They were back down to about $30 a year ago and seem to be heading back up again. Even though the Oil Weapon crisis seems to be over, leaders in Washington should not lose sight of the importance of making North America self-sufficient in energy." During this trip to Calgary, she planned to meet with companies involved in producing crude oil from the massive tar sands and in-situ oil sand resources in north-central Alberta.

She brushed her hair back from the right side of her face and turned to look out the window. *There's the Saddle Dome. Wish the Flames were in town while I'm here. I'll never forget watching Lanny McDonald, Al MacInnis, Joe Nieuwendyk, Mike Vernon, and the rest of the Flames win that Stanley Cup against the Montreal Canadiens in '89.* Her attention swung from the Saddle Dome to the Bow River winding through the middle of town. *Still ice on it. Downtown looks about the same; rush hour looks as bad as ever.*

She thought back to the 1988 Winter Olympics. *It was a warm winter.* She had reported on all of the figure skating and hockey events at the Saddle Dome. *Canadian Olympians won a lot of metals. Brian Orser got silver when Boitano edged him out, Elizabeth Manley was happy to edge out Debbie Thomas for silver when Katarina Witt took gold, and our ice dancing team took bronze.* She had trouble remembering the names of the ice dancing pair. *The final ceremony at McMahon Stadium was something I'll never forget.*

The plane taxied to the arrival gate and stopped. A few minutes later, "Ladies and gentlemen," it was the captain, "the door to the arrival ramp is frozen shut. It'll take them a few minutes to steam it open. Please relax."

Two hours later, Carol and her mother were doing dishes in the kitchen. Her father was in the den watching the eight o'clock news on CBC.

Her mother handed Carol the last of the dinner plates. "We wish U.S. channels would report their thoughts on what Mulroney's doing in Ottawa."

"Americans don't really care what's happening in Canada." Carol dried the plate and put it on top of others in the cupboard. "Most of them don't even know who Mulroney is."

"Politics! You know your dad. He never stops talking about how Ottawa has destroyed western Canada." She knew Carol wanted to discuss some things with her father. "Thanks for helping me clean up, honey. Go in there and talk with your dad about politics. I'll go up to bed and get back into a book I'm reading."

They walked into the den together. He was reading the paper. The TV was on. Her mother went to his chair, leaned over and whispered in his ear. They kissed and he patted her on the butt.

"Probably won't be long," he said to her, before looking up at Carol and throwing the paper to the floor. "Let's talk a while."

"Sure, Dad." Carol turned to her mother. "Sleep well, Mom. It's great to be here."

Her father clicked the television off as her mother left the room.

"Would you like water or something, Dad?"

"No, I'm fine, thanks. Won't be long before I follow your mother. Just want to hear how you're enjoying your responsibilities with TST."

Carol settled into a chair next to him. "Oh, it's wonderful. The people I'm working with are really nice. They work hard, and are sharp! The owner of the station is an older fellow. Name's Adam

Goldsilva, a real hands-on and strong guy who just wants everyone to be at their best at all times. He's had lots of experiences. Kind of reminds me of Uncle Charlie.

"I'm sure you enjoy that atmosphere. What's your responsibility?"

"I'm a research assistant, working with one of the program directors. I'll be in research for at least a year. Might be tried out in front of the camera after that."

"What did you want to discuss?"

"When I was here for the Olympics you mentioned how frustrated western Canadians were with the Mulroney government and how Preston Manning was hoping—"

"Manning's Reform Party is doing well. I think Mulroney's in for a shock in the 1993 election. A lot are really mad about the North American Free Trade Agreement he's negotiating with Reagan and Bush. The Reformers want a new Canada that's got a balanced federation with more equality between provinces."

"I've heard Native groups are—"

"Manning agrees there must be a new deal for Aboriginal Peoples. He also thinks the Senate in Ottawa needs change. And," he chuckled, "that Canada must be workable without Quebec, but attractive enough that the Peasoupers will have a tough time separating."

"Do you think Canada's in trouble?"

He took a while to answer. "I used to love our country, and think it was the greatest nation in the world. We seemed to be on the road to achieving great things until around the late-seventies." He took a deep breath. "Today, it's hard to find anything that really knits our provinces and territories together.

"The economy's in trouble. Our military's depleted and without proper federal commitment. Quebec hasn't even signed-on to our

186

constitution, yet it's still the most influential segment of the country in Ottawa! Powerful business leaders across the country seem more interested in becoming wealthy than in the long-term develop of our country." He shrugged his shoulders. "Frankly, I've lost all respect for most of our corporate and government leaders."

"Do you think—"

"And," he wasn't finished, "the Aboriginals control a lot of our landmass and are restless. And the immigration changes Trudeau forced on us back when he was first elected are creating bothersome pockets of ethnic and religious differences and pressures in most of our major cities."

"Those might—"

He still was not finished. "The only thing saving us right now is the huge nation south of us that needs our resources, some of our manufactured products, and would never let Canada deteriorate too much. God help us if the United States ever decides it no longer needs Canada!"

"So," Carol chuckled, "you think the simple answer to my question is yes?"

He turned to look at her. "What was your question?"

She smiled. "Do you think Canada's in trouble?"

They both laughed.

"I love you, honey." He stood up. "I've got to head up to bed before your mother starts snoring."

During the next several years Carol's career as a television researcher and journalist expanded considerably. She became focused on interviewing people from different countries. In 2004, her schedule took her to Cairo, Egypt. That visit led to a distant love affair that was destined to last for years. But the maverick owner of TST left her little time for a personal life. Adam Goldsilva was continuously pushing and encouraging Carol toward new challenges.

2008

The financial meltdown of Wall Street and the entire U.S. financial system in 2008 hit Goldsilva especially hard.

"No one, no company in America, is too big to fail," he repeated time and again. "That's not capitalism. It's a complete insult to our system. It's a socialism of capitalists, at the expense of the public! Why would Washington bail-out those crooks and cheats?" He was determined to challenge the system.

Within days, he called Carol into his office. The short, stocky, bald, double-chinned TST owner seemed to completely fill the chair on the other side of his paper-loaded desk. The office was small and poorly lit. There were books, magazines, and papers scattered everywhere. And his eyes blinked continuously in reaction to smoke from the cigar stub that seemed permanently stuck in the left corner of his mouth.

"I understand it's a touchy subject, especially here in New York City," he said in reaction to Carol's question. "We have a lot of touchy people here. I don't care about that. We want the truth, not just the politically correct excuses and weak-kneed solutions that are driving this great country into the worst depression it's ever experienced. I hired you and the rest of the gang here because you are problem-solvers and decision-makers, not fault-finders and parrots like those who most Americans enjoy watching for hour after hour!" His grin sent a rush of encouragement and confident adrenalin through Carol. "Just do things the way you normally do, Carol.

Don't worry what those friends of mine might think. I hate what many of them have done, especially their expectations that ordinary Americans should bail them out!"

He reached down to the side of his desk.

"I had our cartoonists think about it and they gave me this." He lifted a black-and-white, two- by three-foot, cardboard-backed poster to his desk, facing Carol. It was an artist's depiction showing the map of the United States and Canada with the southern portion being sucked into a sewer and billion-dollar bills flying off the east coast and across the Atlantic.

"I really like it," Adam said excitedly. "I asked them to give it some colour." He didn't bother to ask Carol's opinion, and instead grabbed a small slip of paper from the top of one of the paper piles on his desk. "Here. That's the name and telephone number of a good friend who's also damn angry with our banks and leaders on Wall Street. Make sure you include Mr. Grumner in your interviews. He'll tell it like it really is."

He wrenched the stub of cigar from his mouth and waved his arm on its way to the loaded ashtray. "Now get out of here and get to work."

Ten days later, a stream of cigar smoke followed Harry Grumner out of Goldsilva's office. Harry was wearing a dark navy suit, white shirt, and paisley tie. He took a deep breath of fresher air. There was a gleam of determination in his dark eyes as he started walking the corridor to Carol's office. He was halfway to Carol's office when she opened the door.

"Mr. Grumner?" Carol held out her hand. "So glad to meet you."

Harry smiled. "Hello, Ms. Fulton. Glad to meet you." They shook hands. "Your boss has asked me to help you get started on a new research project."

Carol gestured for Harry to enter her small and cluttered office, and they settled into chairs across the desk from each other.

"Thanks for coming to see me, Mr. Grumner. I'm trying to find out who's really in control of our monetary system here in America. Who really controls the money supply side of things? The FED? How does Wall Street fit in? And the insurance and brokerage companies? Who really manoeuvres the financial puppet strings in Washington?" She looked into Grumner's eyes. "Can you help me find support for the answers to any of those questions?"

Harry leaned back in the chair, clasped his hands together behind his head, and smiled. "Carol," he said, "many very bright people have been asking questions like that for as long as I can remember, and none I know have had the guts to keep reaching deep enough to expose the real truth." He leaned forward and rested his open hands on the desk. "I'll do whatever I can to help you get there."

Carol grabbed a notebook and pen as Harry kept talking.

CHAPTER 16

A RUSSIAN PERSPECTIVE

Seven years later
Spring 2016; Moscow, Russia

Carol was on her own as she walked briskly up the wide expanse of eight steps to the front door of the dull-grey, main five-storey building that was the entrance to a multiunit retirement care complex in a sparsely developed sector of heavily forested land on the northeast edge of Moscow. She was fifty-two years old. There were heavy traces of gray at the roots of her carelessly groomed red-brown hair and strands twisted haphazardly down the left side of her face and over that eye, some trapped behind the back of her ears and most ending in flowing curls near her neck and shoulders. She was wearing walking shoes with low heels. The warmth of the early afternoon sun penetrated through her multi-coloured blouse and reflected off the concrete steps to warm her legs. She felt dwarfed as she grabbed the large handle and pushed the huge front door. It swung open easily.

Three years earlier, Adam Goldsilva had granted Carol full research and writing independence under a ten-year contract with TST, with a retainer guarantee of $500,000 per year and a minimum payment of $150,000, plus all related expenses, for each documentary used by the multimedia company. Carol welcomed the change because she had always enjoyed covering the other side of important stories and could now define her own priorities and business timetable. Her programs had already covered a wide range of topics, most recently including two documentaries titled *What Will the Coming Election Cycle Mean for America?* and *Is the EU Too Big for Its Britches?* Some of the major media networks in America had tried to persuade Goldsilva to drop Carol because her reports frequently went into depths some considered politically incorrect, discriminatory, or out of bounds in Western journalism; however, the tough, cigar-smoking entrepreneur always resisted those pressures. The purpose of her trip to Moscow was to develop a better perspective of fundamentals behind Russia's recent actions in Ukraine and Syria.

Carol closed the door and walked across the white marble floor to the reception desk. Check-in was fast and orderly. A large and pleasant female attendant who understood little English accompanied Carol to a room on the third floor of the main building and rapped twice on the door. Several seconds later, it slowly opened. A white-bearded face and two dark piercing eyes peeked around the corner, a half foot lower than Carol was expecting.

"Come in, my dear." Yurri Chevanov's eyes widened with joy. He shuffled his feet and opened the door wider. "That will be all," he said to the attendant in Russian. "Thank you." He looked into Carol's eyes and extended his frail right hand. "We can handle things from here," in English, "can't we, my dear?"

This guy's not bad for ninety-six, Carol thought as she walked through the door and made a slight bow toward Yurri. "We certainly can, Mr. Chevanov." She took his hand.

Yurri gripped Carol's hand as he closed the door. "Come," he turned toward his room, "you can help me to the couch over there."

He held tight to Carol's hand as he shuffled across the room and edged his way between the couch and a small coffee table set with a plate of small cookies, a thermos, coffee cups, and small napkins. He stopped, turned slowly, released his grip, and flopped backwards onto the couch. "You sit there." He nodded to the chair at the other side of the table. "Those are my favourite cookies, and there's fresh coffee in the thermos."

"Could I pour you some coffee?" Carol asked as she settled into her chair.

He chuckled. "Not yet, my dear, not yet." Another chuckle. "My bladder can't take much of that stuff anymore. But please, help yourself."

As she poured coffee for herself, Carol recapped what she knew about Yurri Chevanov. *His father and Joseph Stalin were the closest of boyhood friends when they grew up in Gori, Georgia, late in the nineteenth century. They were both raised Greek Orthodox, both worked together in Russia's early oil drilling operations in Siberia, and took part in the 1917 Bolshevik Revolution. When Stalin became general secretary of the Communist Party in 1922, Chevanov's father was at his side, but he disappeared mysteriously soon after Stalin replaced Lenin as leader in 1924. Apparently Stalin had a special liking for his friend's highly intelligent son and saw to Yurri's education, insisting that he study all the single-deity religions and the economic systems in the Western world.* Carol felt pleased she had been able to arrange the meeting. *He's written several books highly respected in Russia.* She searched for Chevanov's eyes somewhere in the bearded face that seemed to be pasted into the large couch without being attached to a body.

Suddenly, a mouthful of small chipped teeth showed in the broad smile that filled the bottom half of his face, and his eyes sparkled. "Well, my dear, what can I do for you?"

Carol took a brief second to gather her thoughts. "Well," she leaned forward to ensure he could hear, "Mr. Chevanov, I would appreciate it very much if you would describe Russia's perspective of what's been happening in your country since the Cold War ended in the early 1990s." She paused. "Especially as it relates to the situations in Ukraine and Syria today."

"That's quite a story." Yurri's voice was surprisingly loud. "It's not complicated, if you know the history of Russia, the Ukraine, and---." He ended with a disinterested and unclear mumble. "Should I start from the beginning?"

Carol nodded. "Yes, of course."

Yurri's right hand shook slightly and his fingers seemed unusually frail as he scratched his furrowed forehead. "Russia is the largest nation in the world. We border many different nations and those borders are almost impossible to effectively defend. Currently, fourteen other sovereign nations share our land borders and two others, the United States, in Alaska, and Japan, share ocean borders with us." He paused, took a deep breath, and swallowed. "Defending our borders is difficult because there aren't many natural geographical boundaries, such as oceans, major river systems, and mountain ranges defining our borders and physically separating us from our neighbours." He struggled for breath. "It has always been quite simple for invaders to cross our land borders, such as the Mongols in 1237, Napoleon and his Frenchmen early in the nineteenth century, and the German armies in the World Wars during the first part of the twentieth century." A quiet sigh was followed by several deep breaths. "We have a great wealth of important natural resources that others wish to control, and we have strong-willed and well educated people."

Yurri pulled at his beard and looked at the tray of small cookies. "Could you give me one of those cookies, my dear?"

Carol reached forward, picked up the plate, and started to extend it to—

"No, please just put one in my mouth."

Carol hesitated, placed the plate back on the table, and picked up one of the small cookies between the tips of her right thumb and forefinger. She stood, braced her feet, and could sense her heart beating faster as she leaned across the table to aim the cookie at Yurri's hair-camouflaged mouth. She stretched further and his head moved forward slowly, his mouth slightly open. Carol wondered if the cookie would fit. Suddenly, Yurri's head lurched forward, his mouth opened wider, the cookie was gone, he settled back into the couch and munched. Carol felt relief as she rubbed her fingers on her skirt and sat back in the chair.

"I understand you were born and raised in Canada," he continued, sending a few cookie crumbs through the air and onto his beard. "That is also a huge country with climatic and logistical challenges similar to ours. But the United States is your only bordering neighbour and it chooses to peacefully control what happens there."

Carol did not want to get off subject. "I understand what you mean."

"Well," he paused, "after Napoleon's defeat and prior to the beginning of the twentieth century, Russia experienced many years of peace under the czarist regime. We had a strong Christian society, Greek Orthodox. And most of our economy was thriving." A deep breath. "Our major cities had some of the most modern and beautiful buildings and infrastructures in the world. During and since the Cold War, some significant changes occurred, driven primarily by those who control world finance."

World finance? Carol thought. "I'm not sure I follow."

Yurri nodded. "I understand your confusion." He cleared his throat. "Do you understand that the Roman and Protestant Christian religions were the fundamental driving force behind modern developments in Western Europe and North America?"

Carol did not respond.

"Well, since the great schism split the Christian teachings, and during the Islamic years of the Ottoman Empire, our Russian society thrived under Greek Orthodox teachings and moralities."

Carol had no idea where he was leading. She grabbed a cookie and started eating while Yurri continued.

"My studies suggest challenges to the moral teachings of the Western churches closely coincided with the development of the grand lodges of Freemasonry from the early 1700s, when wealthy businessmen attempted to rationalize Christian morals with their business objectives. Those churches, the Western Christian ones, eventually stopped stressing some key points of Christian teachings and," he breathed deeply and shook his head, "the bankers now have control over those economies."

What is this? Carol wondered. She said nothing as Chevanov continued.

"The situation in Russia was different. In 1815, at the Congress of Vienna that followed the defeat of Napoleon, Czar Alexander declined Nathan Rothschild's proposal to set up a central bank in Russia." He chuckled. "I expect you're familiar with that famous Rothschild quote." He paused to recall. "'I care not what puppet is placed on the throne. The man who controls Britain's money supply controls the British Empire.'" He shook his head. "Anyway, the czar would have none of that!"

"So, what about in Russia?" Carol asked impatiently. "Are you saying the Rothschild banking system never extended into Russia?"

Yurri thought for a moment. "Today our banking system is run by the state. However, many years ago, a few powerful German-based banks did extend into Russia. I expect most of their representatives living here converted to Christianity, whether they believed in it or not." He paused. "But there was an event that occurred late in the eighteenth century, not long before the Napoleonic War. It is unique to Russia. Do you know what that was?"

Carol was not listening closely and was surprised by the question. "What?"

Yurri smiled. "I understand, my dear. Some of this stuff can be boring. But I think it's important for you to understand."

"What was your question?" Carol asked impatiently.

"Do you know anything about the Pale of Settlement?"

"I've heard of it." She was totally disinterested. "Why is it unique?"

"In 1791, Catherine the Great decided that most Jews who did not convert to Christianity and follow Christian morals should live in a special area in the western part of the country. The Pale kept expanding, mostly through a series of border conquests against Prussia and the 1793 partition of Poland. After the defeat of Napoleon, there was an even greater Jewish population in the Pale. Probably close to fifty per cent of the world Jewish population lived there." He paused to breathe. "Did I mention that the German banker Rothschild wanted to establish a central bank in Russia at that time?"

"Yes, you did." Carol's interest was building. "But, let me ask, why did the Russian rulers isolate the Jewish people?"

Yurri shrugged. "It always just seems to happen. A case of different morals and behaviours, I guess. The ancestors of many of the Jews in the Pale had previously been exiled from Britain, France, Spain, Portugal, and other nations. At least in the Pale, they could practice their own ways and were under the protection of Russia."

"But—I know I've heard this from others—wasn't the Pale of Settlement a serious limitation against Jewish freedoms?"

Yurri chuckled. "That's an abstraction." He saw the puzzlement in Carol's eyes. "You know what I mean by an abstraction, I'm sure. Western journalists use abstractions all the time during their five-second explanations of things." He didn't wait for eye contact. "Abstractions sound good, smart; but it's really a way the speaker has of avoiding details, and the devil is always in the details." He finally had eye contact. "But, my dear, yours is a good question and it deserves a thoughtful answer, not just another abstraction." He smiled. "Give me a moment so I can try to shape my response with the best wisdom I can drum up right now." He paused for only a few seconds. "Listen. Devout Jews have something like 613 commandments and laws they must follow. If that isn't enough to make them feel freedom-less, I don't know what is!" He smiled at the simplicity and bluntness of his remark. "The truth is, in the Pale, they were completely free to practice their ways without interference with others." He smiled. "That's the best answer I can give you."

"Well—" Carol had no idea what to say.

"But, we shouldn't get off track," Yurri said. "Let me continue with our Russian history." He seemed to have found a second wind, and Carol tried to refocus as he continued.

"I already mentioned that the nineteenth century was a great time in Russian history. However, by late in that century, the czarist government was losing perspective. There began a socialist groundswell and Nicholas II was not properly trained to lead the nation when he became czar in 1894 at the age of twenty-six. The 1904–05 war with Japan and World War One were extremely damaging and disruptive to the nation. There was a revolution and Bolsheviks came to dominate our government." Yurri started coughing and began to gag.

Carol jumped up and patted him on the back. After a couple of minutes, he settled back.

"Thanks, my dear." Yurri gathered his breath. "That seems to be happening to me more and more. Old age, I guess." He paused and looked up at Carol. "Maybe I should have a sip of coffee."

Carol leaned over and poured some coffee into Yurri's cup. She looked at him and pointed questioningly to the milk and sugar. He smiled and nodded. She added both and started stirring.

Yurri could not wait. "Please, just hold it to my lips," he said impatiently.

She stood, leaned forward, and carefully aimed an edge of the cup toward the area of beard where his lips should be. The beard parted slightly, she sensed his lips on the cup and started to cautiously tip. He started slurping loudly. She kept tipping and he kept slurping. Finally, he stopped and signalled with his eyes that he'd had enough. When she took the cup back from his lips, small streams of coffee dribbled down his beard. Carol grabbed a napkin and tapped them dry.

There was a wide smile on Yurri's face and his eyes sparkled with delight. "Thank you, my dear. That was so good. Not like vodka, but close." He chuckled at his little joke.

Carol put the cup and napkin on the table and settled back into her chair.

"You asked about what's happening in Ukraine today and perhaps I should comment on that now," Yurri said.

Finally! Carol thought as he continued.

"Throughout modern times, the Ukraine has always been a fundamental and important part of Russia, even though there were times it operated as a separate nation. Along with Poland and other areas, it had a large Jewish population. After the First World War, many Jews emigrated to the British Mandate in Palestine, as well as to the United States and Canada." He paused. "You might want to do some of your own research on that Aliyah because it has a great deal to do with how those areas are governed today.

"Many years later, at the end of the Cold War, Russia's military and industrial complex was quite chaotic and Boris Yeltsin, who replaced Gorbachev, lacked political will. Thankfully, that changed in 2000, when Vladimir Putin took control. Putin reorganized the military to ensure protection of our homeland and its resources. He is what I call a true guardian of our nation." Yurri sat forward on the couch with his palms on his knees, his eyes intensified, and his voice became louder. "But NATO, primarily at the prodding of America and the international banking network, kept encroaching into regions that had been in Russia's sphere of influence for hundreds of years. Encroachment into the affairs of Ukraine was just too much. Beyond insult!" He rested back and threw his frail arms in the air. "And now we've got those crazy U.S. sanctions against our country. Few goyim in the West have any idea of what's really happening."

"Can you prove—?"

"My dear," Yurri swiftly interrupted, "one only needs to go back to the beginning to properly understand what's been happening. Thankfully, our leadership in Russia is not stupid and—"

Carol was losing patience and without thinking, she blurted, "What about Russia's brutality against Mr. Browder and his investment fund?"

Yurri did not react, as if he had not heard her. There was a long silence. Carol finally tried to make eye contact but Yurri's eyes were closed. The awkward silence continued for another couple of minutes. Finally, Carol shifted in her seat and cleared her throat in hopes of waking him.

Yurri opened his eyes and smiled. He laughed. "I wasn't asleep, my dear. I was trying to recall the details of that Hermitage affair. I'm sure your American papers and Washington politicians told you all a much different story than what really happened right here in Moscow."

"Oh?"

He nodded. "Really. That Hermitage Fund used its access to international investments, mostly Jewish, in an effort to transfer great wealth, trillions of rubles and billions of U.S. dollars, out of Russia. It interfered with our government's effort to transfer ownership in major government corporations to ordinary Russian citizens. The government could not let that happen."

Carol remembered only some of the details she had recently read in the book titled *Red Notice*. "Washington saw it differently. The Magnitsky Act is behind those sanctions."

Yurri looked bored, suddenly tired. He nodded. "I know all about that. It's a great example of how easily Zionists sway the whole scope of activity in Washington." He laughed.

"What do you mean? I don't—"

"My dear, that whole affair was a result of a scheme by wealthy investors, mostly from America, Israel, and parts of Western Europe—maybe even Canada. The organizer of the scheme planned to transfer billions of dollars out of Russia and into the hands of billionaires in the West. Our government could not let that happen. And now, because that thievery was caught, Washington is throwing sanctions at Russia from all over the place!" He took several deep breathes. "Someday, Americans will wake up and understand what's really happening!" He coughed softly. "If you want some insight into what I mean, read the Protocols of Zion." Emotional saliva rushed into his mouth and dripped onto his beard. After a couple of swallows he rubbed the back of his right hand across his beard. "Understand, my dear, Ukraine is important to Russia and," he slapped open palms down on his thighs, "we are determined to stop Western aggression from getting too close." He took a deep breath and closed his eyes.

He's fading quickly. Don't dare mention Syria. Carol cleared her throat. "That's all very interesting, Mr. Chevanov." She wondered if he heard her.

Yurri grunted and managed a weak chuckle as he opened his eyes. "I wish you the best of luck in your search." He coughed, wiped his hand across his mouth, swallowed hard, and held out his hands.

"Could you please help me up? I will walk you to the door. Then I need to take a nap."

They were halfway to the door when Yurri stopped abruptly, turned, and looked into Carol's eyes. "I must comment upon the beauty of your eyes, my dear. They are full of life and honesty." As abruptly, he turned and continued walking to the door.

Ten minutes later, Carol settled into the back seat of the taxi. As it started moving, she took a note pad and pencil from a small pocket on the right side of her skirt.

That was some interview! A whole different perspective on things. I've got to check and confirm a lot of what he said. She noted a couple of points. *Some things seem connected with points Tariq has mentioned.* She looked out the window at the golden tops of the Kremlin buildings far in the distance. *I need to read those protocols.*

CHAPTER 17

COMA DREAMS

Two months later
July 2016; New York City

It was 8:30 p.m. on Sunday evening. Carol had the dinner dishes in the dishwasher and felt bushed. *Cleaning the apartment was a lot of work. I'm ready to hit the sack after an e-mail to Tariq.* She walked slowly into her small office, flopped into the desk chair, opened her computer and e-mail server, and started typing.

> *Hello Honey,*
>
> *Hope all is well with you. I think of you always.*
> *It's been a busy week here, with our presidential election campaign in full swing. You've probably been watching how our major networks are turning it into a real partisanship free-for-all. November 8 is bound to be a big day here in America. I'm determined to not get caught up in all the mudslinging and to report only the facts and stay impartial—which might be difficult! I can see a smile on your face.*
> *Of course, we aren't the only nation with serious political issues. The Brexit decision will impact the future of*

*the EU for many years and the radical jihad in Iraq
and Syria is forcing too many Muslim people into
Western nations. On that last item, I have no idea what
to say regarding the long-term consequences. It's hope-
lessly confusing to me. Any advice you can give?*

*I recently read a publication that tried to explain
"Europe's Chronic Jihadist Problem." It suggested
the "roots of radicalization" started long ago with the
Umayyad invasion of Spain and France in the 700s
and continued through the Christian Crusades in the
1200s, the Ottoman surges of Vienna in the 1500s and
1600s, the European colonization of North Africa and
South Asia in the 1700s and 1800s, and the fall of
the Ottoman Empire and European colonization of
the Middle East after WWI. It also pointed out how
Muslims have moved to Europe in search of education
and employment but generally failed to be effectively
integrated into those societies. It's all quite confusing
and I still feel no wiser.*

I'm almost asleep. Looking forward to seeing you soon.

Love,

Carol

Five months later
Late December 2016; Calgary, Alberta

The WestJet flight from New York's Kennedy Airport circled north
before turning to make its final descent to the Calgary International
Airport. *That's Airdrie, really spread out now*, Carol thought as she
looked out her window on the right side of the plane. The outskirts

of Calgary were immediately in sight and she began to pick out familiar landmarks. *Mom says most downtown office buildings are half empty owing to the recession caused by low oil prices.* She looked toward the mountains. *Sun's almost gone! No clouds. Those snow-capped mountains are beautiful!* A couple of minutes later she heard the landing gear lock and suddenly the mountains were almost lost against the darkening sky. As the plane taxied to the terminal, Carol's anticipation focused on her parents. *They're both in good health, but I think Dad's getting bored. He's talking about maybe moving to the coast or BC interior. This might be the last time I see the house.* The check-through at Canadian customs was fast and her parents were waving excitedly when she walked into the crowded airport lobby.

During the drive from the airport to the house in west Calgary, the conversation turned to the excitement and turmoil associated with Donald Trump's preparations for becoming president of the United States in less than a month. "I'm sure you're steeped in what's happening," Carol's father said as he guided the Lexus 460 through heavy rush-hour traffic on some slippery roads. "Let's have a drink and talk about it when we get home."

"Good idea," Carol agreed.

"I think it's just a big mess!" her mother said in a discouraged voice. "I'll get things ready for tomorrow while the two of you talk about that stupid spectacle."

Carol and he father talked late into the evening. Her mother had gone to bed.

"Well," her father concluded, "about all we know for sure is that Americans have some interesting and challenging years ahead. It'll be fun to see if he manages to clean out the swamp in Washington."

"We'll see after he gets into the White House on January 20." Carol yawned and rubbed her eyes.

"I'm bushed, too," he father said. "Let's hit the sack before Santa gets here."

Christmas morning at the Fulton house was pretty much the same as always. Carol and her mother spent more than an hour in the kitchen preparing the eighteen-pound turkey. Her father spent some time outside clearing newly fallen snow from the sidewalks and porches. When he finished outside, it was time for him to put the heavily loaded roaster into the 320-degree preheated oven. It was about 1:00 in the afternoon when they gathered in the front room to open presents by the Christmas tree.

Later that evening, Carol and her father were sitting alone in the den. Her mother had gone to bed.

"What a wonderful day," Carol sighed. She yawned. "There's nothing like Mom's Christmas dinner."

"Wish you didn't have to leave tomorrow. We'd love you to stay a few more days, honey."

"I know, Dad. Wish I could, but I'm pursuing a story that's got me going in a bunch of different directions, and I've finally arranged a key interview for the twenty-seventh in New York."

"What's the story?" he asked. "On the new presidency?"

"Maybe. I guess. Indirectly." She paused. "Mr. Goldsilva got a couple of us together in his office a few months ago and said if Trump is committed to making America great again, we should try and document what exactly caused us to lose that greatness."

"Interesting. A good point." Something came to his mind. "You know, that reminds me of a good book I read a couple of months ago called *The War That Ended Peace*. It was written by one of our best Canadian authors, Margaret MacMillan. It outlined the state of things, especially the political confusions, misdirections and," he searched for the best word, "complete arrogance and hubris of many leaders in the major nations of Europe in the years leading up to the First World War." He looked into his daughter's eyes. "You know, as I was reading it, I couldn't help thinking we might be in a similar situation today."

"I haven't heard anything about that book," Carol said. "What did MacMillan say about the Zionist movement back at the end of the nineteenth century?"

Her father drew a blank. He scratched his head and looked up to his left, trying to recall. "I don't recall much being said about that. Maybe it wasn't really important. Why?"

Hmm, interesting. "Oh, nothing really, except the Zionist movement was a powerful new political force throughout the Western world at that time. I would have expected—" She paused. "Have you still got the book? Could I look through it tonight?"

"It's about six hundred pages!"

"That's okay." She chuckled. "I've become a good speed reader. Besides, I just want to check for a couple of things and I can probably look through the index."

"It's in the library." He braced his hands on the arms of the chair and stood up. "I'll get it for you."

While he was gone, Carol reflected on how good it had been to spend Christmas with her parents. She looked up and smiled as he came back into the room with the book in his hand. "That *is* a big book!" *I'm anxious to see what it says.*

He handed it to her. "I'm heading to bed. Have fun with your speed reading." He bent over and kissed her forehead. "Love you, honey."

The next morning, Carol and her parents left the house at 10:30. Her father drove and the ladies were in the back seat. The WestJet flight to New York was scheduled to depart Calgary International Airport at 1:10 p.m. The ladies chatted about old friends as they passed different neighbourhoods. Then their discussion turned to clothes and how thrilled each was that everything they received for Christmas fit. By the time the car turned onto eastbound Memorial Drive, they seemed to be out of things to talk about.

Carol's father broke the silence. "What did you think of that book you looked at last night?"

"I'm glad I scanned it. It's sure a thorough documentation of many points of history." She spoke loudly to ensure he could hear. "But, truthfully, I was taken by some important things it didn't mention."

He was focused on his driving. When he stopped for the red light at Edmonton Trail, he asked, "What do you mean? What do you think was left out?"

Carol leaned forward a bit. "Like we touched on last night—" She looked at her mom as if to say, *Should I be distracting him while he's driving?* Her mom waved her arm in a don't-worry manner, and Carol continued. "Probably one of the most powerful new political movements throughout the Western part of the world was only given a passing mention. I found that strange, especially given where my research has taken me and the detailed nature of that book on so many other things."

The light changed and the Lexus jumped ahead of the other traffic. As they passed the Calgary Zoo, he said, "I remember wondering while reading the book, why all those nations that seemed at the peak of enjoyment back at the end of the nineteenth century would suddenly experience so much turmoil." He shook his head. "It was sure a lot more peaceful than we have it today!"

Carol said nothing as her father turned the car onto the off-ramp from Memorial Drive and got up to speed with the heavy 110-kph traffic going north on Deerfoot Trail.

"Oh," Carol's mother offered, "I read someplace a long time ago that the world bankers made billions from their loans to each warring nation. They never worried about which side was good or bad, just loaned money to whoever wanted it." She turned and looked at Carol. "Is that what you're talking about?"

"That's maybe part of it, Mom." Carol shifted her attention back to her dad. "It just struck me as rather strange that there was no mention in the book of how really significant the Zionist movement was at that time."

"Maybe I should read up on that Zionist stuff," her father said. "I've always thought of it as kind of a hush-hush topic. Any books you'd recommend?"

Carol thought for a moment. "Read *The Controversy of Zion* if you're interested. It's written by," she paused and took a pen and paper from her purse. "I'll write it down for you, Dad." She wrote, *Controversy of Zion* by Geoffrey Wheatcroft. "And there's a more recent book you should read," she continued as she wrote, *Our Promised Land* by Charles Selengut. She handed the paper to her mother.

The Lexus swerved for no apparent reason.

"Are you okay, Dad?" Carol reacted.

"Yah," he wiped his brow and rubbed his eyes, "just got something in my eye. Sorry. What were you saying?" The Lexus quickly recovered to 110 kph.

"I wrote the titles for you. Mom has it. The best books I've read about the start-up of the Zionist movement and the reactions of various Jewish people throughout the world."

The car swerved again, this time to the left. Cars behind and to the left honked their horns.

"Are you okay, Dad?" Carol was suddenly concerned.

"Yah, I think so," he said in a frightened voice. They were still travelling at high speed. "I'll check Amazon for a cheap copy."

"Slow down, dear," Carol's mother ordered loudly. She looked at Carol. "I really don't like all this talk about Zionists and Jews. What happened to Christianity? Why has—"

A horn blared as the Lexus swung abruptly into the lane on the right. Carol's father fell forward against the steering wheel, unconscious. They were still travelling at 110 kph. A large semitrailer slammed into the side of the Lexus, crushing her mother to Carol's side and flipping the Lexus high in the air. More horns were blaring. A car hit the front of the Lexus, spinning it in the other direction before it flipped again and landed upside-down as an explosion ripped the car apart.

We're all dead, Carol thought as warm blood poured over her face and she sensed a small part of her gut tearing away from her numb body. A brilliant white light flashed as her mother's question lingered in her mind.

Flames and smoke rose high in the cold Calgary air.

Twenty-four hours later

"What happened to Christianity?!"

Her mother's last words raced through Carol Fulton's comatose brain.

Two nurses were changing shifts. They turned in reaction to the buzz alert on the monitor. "Her brain's alive!" both exclaimed as one, as they saw new blips on the screen monitoring Carol's brainwaves.

Carol's brain had been inactive since arrival at the Lougheed General Hospital less than an hour after the car accident. She had no idea she was in a hospital bed with her entire body wrapped in various casts and bandages, a breathing tube in her nose, and brain probes in her bandaged head. Her heart was strong and operating normally, and she was breathing on her own through the hose from an oxygen machine at the side of the bed. Her broken right leg was in a full-length cast supported in the air by a sling raised above bed level, and her burns, all considered nonthreatening, were covered. She was restrained by straps to ensure any unassisted movement was limited to the ends of her fingers. The nurses had witnessed similar situations before and correctly assumed her brain was essentially dead, until now.

"She might be a lucky lady, after all," said the outgoing nurse.

"Maybe," the other agreed. "Who knows what those brainwaves mean? It may be nothing, or it could be something encouraging. Who knows? Our brains are so—I don't know how to say it—connected to our souls, to our spirits."

What's she talking about? her colleague wondered. "I guess. We've sure seen some unbelievable things over the years, haven't we?" She turned to leave. "Good luck during your shift."

Carol could not hear what the nurses were saying. However, a familiar voice was clear in her coma-dream. "You're safe, honey." Carol recognized the voice but saw only a bright white light surrounding her. "Mother?" she reacted. "Yes, dear. Our spirits are with you, your father and I."

Carol dropped into a contented and dreamless sleep, the monitors returned to normal, and the nurse took her favourite book from the shelf before settling into a chair at the side of Carol's bed. She had no idea that Carol's coma-dreams would become a regular thing during the coming hours and days.

"My god!" exclaimed the nurse several days later as the monitor beeped wildly. She reached to push the emergency button. Before she could press the button, the monitors returned to normal. *I'll just watch for a moment*, she decided.

Hours later, Carol was in another coma-dream. "I Am here with you." "God?" "Yes, Carol." "I can't see you." "You see Me everywhere, everywhere there is life." Carol slept.

The dreams continued.

"How's Ms. Fulton doing?" the surgeon asked as he walked into the room. "I was thinking about her during the Phoenix conference."

"I bet you were!" The nurse smiled as she turned to look into his eyes. "That's a great suntan you've got. How was the golf?"

"Good. Really good. And the weather was perfect." He was at the bedside. "Any improvement?"

"Her vital signs are all strong. I have the feeling she could break out of her coma any time. We keep testing her sense of touch and hearing but no indications yet. At times, I sense she's enjoying where she is."

"That's not her option," the doctor said authoritatively as he turned to leave. "Give me a call if she starts coming out of it."

Carol had no idea that her private hospital room was taking on the look and fragrance of a flower shop with bouquets and Get Well cards from concerned friends and admirers. And different subjects, ones that had been burnt into her subconscious as a result of the research, speculation, and imagination she had experienced over the past year began to surface in her coma-dreams; coming and going without any clear pattern.

"I control our empire." The stranger's steel-blue eyes made her cringe. "You can be one of us, if you obey."

She moved! The attending nurse felt sure she had seen Carol's little finger move. She looked up at the monitor. *More brain activity, really active!* She put her book down and gave Carol closer attention, completely unaware of the coma-dreams.

"Join my wife and I for dinner," ordered the man. Carol focused on a small z-shaped monogram near the tip of the left collar of his shirt. "We pray first. Listen carefully to me." It seemed she had no choice but to obey, and several dreams blended into one. "Our forefathers came from another galaxy. Best results in governing earth are attained by violence and terrorism. We monopolize trade and industry through ownership of gold, land and control of money. Everything is to be settled by the question of figures and statistics." Carol wanted to run but she couldn't. "As rulers here we covet all and utilize cunning and make believe; frankness and honesty are vices in earth's politics. We are atheist and accept no religions. We favour Judaism; that tribe is faithful, widespread and valuable as our collectors and administrators, and scapegoats whenever needed. Christian goyim are ignorant and bemused with alcohols, amusements,

215

passions, palaces and other distractions; they are wandering sheep and we are the wolves; they will accept money as the predominant first of their fruits." Carol's trembling was undetectable. "War is necessary but must never be for territorial gain; it is our leverage for control and both sides are at the mercy of our agents; it is the only solution against Islam. Democratic governments are pawns in our hands; we limit terms of leaders, select judiciary and control courts of law, control their financial systems, all key policies are from our administrators; we control the free press and all media, thereby all education." He stopped his devotion, opened his eyes and smiled across the table at Carol.

"Help! Save me!" Carol tried to shout. The monitor alarm buzzed loudly. The nurse pushed the emergency button and watched in disbelief as Carol's eyes popped wide open, then closed.

"What's happening?" The floor supervisor rushed into the room. The alarm was still buzzing.

The bed nurse gasped for breath. "She opened her eyes!"

"Impossible."

"I'm hungry," Carol's eyes were open again and her lips were quivering.

CHAPTER 18

A BROADWAY PLAY: *"GREAT AGAIN"*

Several days later

It took Carol two days to fully understand and accept what had happened. By the fifth day, her day nurses were reading Get Well messages to her. Carol could think only of her parents. *I feel they're fine, right here with me.*

The nurse finished reading a card from Tariq. "Mr. Radwan called yesterday and asked us to let him know as soon as you can have visitors." Carol smiled and dropped into a peaceful sleep.

Ten days later, Tariq was at her side. All monitoring equipment had been removed from the room and the only bandage visible beyond the bedcovers was the cast on her right leg, which rested normally on the bed. Carol's hair was mostly dull grey, her eyebrows and eyelashes only shadows starting to grow back in. Her body was marked by blotches of red where the skin was still healing from burns.

"I can't remember anything after Dad's head fell to the steering wheel and we hit the first car," Carol explained to Tariq. "Mom and I were in the back seat." She shook her head. "They were both so—"

"I'm sorry, dear," Tariq said. "Their souls—"

217

"Somehow I feel they're still with me."

She recovered remarkably fast. Two months after the accident, she was out of the hospital, in a walking cast, living in her parent's home and more determined than ever to find answers to the puzzle that had been unfolding with more and more clarity prior to her trip to Calgary. She could remember only scattered pieces of subjects that kept jumping in and out of her mind. *Russian history. The European Union. The world banking system. Something about Zionism. But why are all those things racing around in my mind?*

She finally decided to ask Tariq, the day before he was returning to Cairo. "Tariq, do you know what the focus of my research was before the accident?"

"I think so. You seemed focused on a couple of things."

"What?"

"One thing has been concerning most of the world for some time now: the possibility of a major war breaking out at any time. North Korea, Ukraine, Syria, Afghanistan are all serious tinder boxes right now. And," he snickered, "nobody has any idea how President Trump intends to use his art-of-the-deal talents and the power of the CIA and Pentagon."

Carol nodded. "I think I'm probably up to speed on that issue. It's really wait and see. What was the other thing?"

Tariq didn't answer immediately. "Not sure I can describe that very well. Best I understood was that you felt a lot of the direction and authority of Western nations seemed hidden, like there was some uncovered level of supervision, authority, and direction that was above and beyond that of governments."

"Where would I get that from?"

"Not sure." It was a half-truth because he did not want her to get excited. "It might have been a combination of things. Frankly, the EU is an ideal example of that concern, and the Brexit vote might have been what brought the whole thing to a head in your mind. I know you were researching NATO and the UN in an effort to understand the decision-making processes and authorities there, and the election of Trump to the White House was maybe---" He shrugged.

"I'm remembering more each day. Maybe there'll be more answers for me when I get back to the office in New York."

"I'm sure there will, dear." He stood up. "What would you like me to make us for dinner?"

Three months later
March 2017; New York City

Carol was glad to see the Manhattan skyline as her flight from Calgary began its descent to Kennedy International Airport; at exactly the same time the American Airline Boeing 787 was taking off for San Diego with Troy and Donna Rogers settled comfortably in first class.

Donna looked out the window at the Statue of Liberty glistening in the last rays of evening sun. "The past four days have been the best time I've ever had in New York," she thought aloud.

"I'm glad we came," Troy agreed. "That fine memorial service, the fun evening with Harry and Rebecca, and we never seem to tire of seeing Phantom. Just hanging around Lincoln Center at noontime today was fun."

The plane had levelled out and the flight attendant brought their drinks.

"I really enjoyed poking along 6th Avenue yesterday. Prices are ridiculous, but quality can't be beat. It's fun to see all the new styles, even if they aren't for me." She sipped her drink. "Did you and Harry solve any problems at the bar?"

Troy sipped his martini. "Sure did. And we both agree this year is critical for Trump and the nation."

"That reminds me of something I read in an old book store just off 6th Avenue. Made me think of Trump's insistence that he's not interested in military conflict with other nations."

"What's that?"

"An old philosopher's saying about being a good general."

"What's that?"

She paused to remember. "A good general, daring to march, dares also to halt, and will never press triumph beyond need."

Troy nodded. "That's good."

"There's more: what he must do is not for glory, not for show, not for self, only because it has to be done." She paused. "I thought that was worth remembering."

"That's good," Troy repeated. "Hope it describes Trump. And hope that advice will still work in our atomic and high-tech age."

They sipped their drinks in silence. "What do you think will happen?" Donna asked.

"It depends. Harry and I both think Trump must follow through on his election promises. He can't get thrown off track by our media or international pressures. Focusing on America first will be key. That's what he promised." Troy sipped his martini. "He can't be expected to do it alone." He set his glass on the tray. "Funny, on the way back to the hotel after lunch I had a sudden revelation when I saw the great crowd in Times Square."

"What?"

"All those different people, going in all different directions, all feeling quite free to do whatever they felt like doing. I sensed that our obsession with freedom might make Trump's task impossible."

She turned and looked at him. "What do you mean?"

"I expect most of the thousand souls I saw in Times Square felt free. But I bet few felt any commitment or determination to improve the economy, help drain the lobby swamp in Washington, help get hundreds of thousands back to work at good paying jobs," he paused for breath, "help stop the inflow of drugs and illegal immigrants from Mexico, ensure that Middle East terrorism has absolutely no chance of breeding in America, or help fix some of the other stuff needed to truly make the country great again." He licked his lips and scratched an itch on his left ear. "And it struck me—"

Donna reached over, held his hand and played with his wedding ring and the large knuckle of his ring finger. "What?"

"Patriotism. We need to redefine American patriotism if we hope to ever switch things back in the right direction. Frankly, that may be impossible, given our obsession with the thought of unlimited freedom. Right now, patriotism seems unimportant."

She leaned toward him, pulled his arm, and they kissed.

"Nothing's more important, other than family. Nothing's more important than patriotism, surely?" She paused and softly chuckled. "Maybe you should write a book about all this stuff. You know, explain how the good men and women we elect to protect and manage the nation so quickly become caught up in partisanship issues. Try to explain what drives our leaders to focus so much attention on international issues that reach well beyond keeping America safe." She slapped her hands down hard on the tray table and turned to him. "Honey, do it. Write a book. Make it a novel. Title it something like," she paused, "*Where Are We Going?* or *What Happened to Us?*

Troy felt a laugh, but it would not come out. He turned and looked at her. "Americans don't care about that stuff anymore." His voice was serious. "I'm better off spending my time relaxing in the backyard and on the golf course."

He rested his head back and closed his eyes, *Patriotism or balkanization: those are probably the only long-term options. Quite the challenge we've created for our descendants!*

Manhattan

About the same time, Carol was opening the door of her condo apartment in Manhattan. *It feels so good to be back. I can hardly wait to see the gang at TST.* She had the weekend to get settled, then back to the office for the first time in three months.

It did not take Adam Goldsilva long to realize Carol's recovery was far from complete. He was not one to push against reality, particularly when his own money was involved, and he considered it impractical to encourage Carol to resume her journalistic career. He had been developing an idea for a new project, a Broadway play, one he hoped might awake Americans from what he often described as 'a complete meltdown of our nation's soul'. The more he thought about it, the more he was convinced that Carol was perfectly suited to take on the task he had in mind. No travel was required, and Adam was hopeful that challenging her inquisitive and determined nature would assist in her recovery.

They were in his cluttered and smoke-filled office, a week after Carol's return.

"Carol, I want you to create a Broadway play that's a mirror on our country. It's time Americans saw a scorecard on how we've handled the principles of democracy and capitalism, and how well we've administered the intents of our Constitution. I expect, inevitably, it will be a polemic satire, an eye-opener. If you can make it light and comical enough, I think Americans will flock to see it."

Carol accepted the challenge. It involved a significant cut in guaranteed remuneration, hopefully to be offset by a substantial percentage of any royalties that might be realized out of a successful Broadway play. And she was excited about getting close to live theatre on Broadway. As things turned out, it was a long and difficult grind, and Goldsilva was not always a patient man.

Three years later
March 2020 New York

It was late afternoon, mid-week. Both Carol and Goldsilva looked and felt worn out as they faced each other across the desk in his office. A heavy rain had been pounding against the office window throughout their ninety minute meeting, and it seemed to be getting worse. Carol was fifty-five years old. Most people who knew him thought Adam should have retired years ago. But nothing could dampen the bright spark of enthusiasm filling the office as they each closed their individual copies of Carol's 120-page screenplay manuscript. On the cover of each copy were large capital letters, A BROADWAY PLAY: *"GREAT AGAIN"*.

"Great job, Carol." Adam took a deep breath as he tapped the manuscript with his left hand. "This is exactly what I had in mind."

"Thanks. Glad you like it."

"Like it!? I'm going to be the proudest man in Manhattan for the rest of my life. Can't think of anything better that we could have done for this country. Now to get it on Broadway. That's my job. I've been prepping important contacts, and it could happen by the end of September." He smiled. "That's before the November election, and we should have them lining up to get tickets."

"Fun. Let me know how I can help."

Adam had cleared his desk before their meeting started, and it was still uncluttered. The only things on the desk were their copies of the manuscript and a clean ashtray. Out of respect he had not lit up his cigar during the meeting. But his constant chewing and spitting into the waste basket to the right of his chair had created a stub that was hardly visible in the corner of his mouth, and there was an unusual odor coming from the basket.

He picked his copy of the manuscript up in both hands, tilted his chair back, and smiled as his feet left the floor and he looked up at the ceiling. "It'll be a hit, I just know it. You've done a great job," he repeated. "And I love the title." His chair came upright. "Another wakeup call from Broadway."

Carol wiggled on her thinly cushioned chair to ease a numbness in her behind. "Most of the critical thoughts, the background for character dialogues, come from your wisdom and foresight, Adam," she complimented. "Things you've said to me from time to time throughout my career, and especially since I started this project. Thanks for letting me be a part of it."

He chuckled. "Maybe that's why I like it so much." He put the manuscript back on the desk. "But clearly, Carol, you did a lot of research; as usual." He tugged the cigar stub from his mouth and threw it into the waste basket. "Thanks for your compliment, but I detected other influences in almost every scene. A couple of times I could visualize Harry Grumner on the stage."

He pulled open the top right drawer of his desk and took out a fresh cigar. "It's clear, you got input from some good patriots; that was wise and fundamental to success." He shifted in the chair to grab a lighter from the left pocket of his pants, put the cigar in his mouth, looked at Carol and smiled. His eyes brightened with delight as he lit the cigar and puffed deeply several times.

Carol stood up and stretched. She was about to turn and leave the office when Adam started to recount key elements of her play.

"It covers a long time period; over thirty years, to at least 2050. Good idea, and really the only way to fit all those scenes into a logical sequence."

He paused, thinking of the sequence.

"China and Russia putting the stop on North Korea's nuclear program was a necessary starting point. It gave the Pentagon the opportunity to get most of our forces out of the Asian theatre, and to focus on things here at home. I think your depiction of a ten-year battle with the NRA, banks, and Wall Street is all probably close to reality. And," he smiled, "the way you involve the Pentagon; that will get people thinking!" There was a grin on his face. "How did you ever come up with the idea of putting the Pentagon leadership in the hands of a lady? She's given quite the power." He looked into Carol's eyes. "That dialogue was really brilliant."

Carol smiled. "It was fun. I thought putting her in charge of the Pentagon during the battle with the NRA will be an audience grabber, result in women wanting to see the play. I'm sure it'll create a lot of controversy, so I made it as comical as I could."

He chuckled, then changed topics.

"I liked how you brought back the Gold Standard and made utilities out of the banks."

Carol had returned to her chair.

"Carol, your characters are so realistic." His eyes brightened. "Those Congressional debates you created in the 2040s; hilarious! The way you've captured the original intents of the Founding Fathers, and brought those intents into the context of complexities today; quite something. And," he took the cigar out of his mouth, "the way you dealt with the old-boy lobbyists in the Capitol was fair; tough but fair." The cigar went back into the left corner of his smiling mouth. "Lobbyists who see the play might have a tough time ever showing up in the Capitol again."

There was an awkward pause.

"Carol, you'll challenge everyone, even me, with that dialogue centred on the First Amendment. It starts simply, innocently, and without any warning your characters start talking about how all good human souls simply seek a social framework where they can live in peace and opportunity; how that's all they really need their leaders to provide. And, right there, you introduced that the leaders have only two options, capitalism or socialism. I can't believe how quickly and clearly you showed that socialism's economic model places overwhelming responsibility for effective management and execution upon the leaders of society." Adam's mind was racing through the simple logic of the scene in the play. "Capitalism, simply making the resources of a society accessible to the innovative and risk-taking imaginations of all citizens, is much easier on the leaders and will provide greater benefit to all, provided taxing methods encourage individual initiative and ensure proper sharing of the benefits realized from the use of society's resources; a much easier chore for leaders. You made it all sound so logical."

"Provided it's a society of properly educated souls seeking peace and opportunity," Carol reminded him.

"I got that, loud and clear. Audiences will be hushed during the senator's speech on the First Amendment, how it only works if the religions referenced in the Amendment are ones that reflect the fruits of the Holy Spirit." Adam took a deep break. "It became quite the debate."

"I wish there'd been more time for that debate," Carol reacted.

"The message is clear." His voice cracked and smoke clouded his eyes as he wiggled in his chair. "I'm keeping you too long." A deep breath. "Enjoying it too much."

He cleared his throat, twice.

"Just one last thought. I'm glad you decided to leave out reference to Canada, Israel, and other nations. North Korea needed to be handled, but the essence of our problems is right here; how we think about ourselves and govern our own communities and lives, right here in America."

"Trying to include those other issues would have been too overwhelming." She could hardly wait to get to the washroom.

"Once *"GREAT AGAIN"* is on Broadway, you can get started on those other stories. I remember you telling me a few years back that your father and uncle thought Canada was slowly going back to the natives and in danger of splitting into cultural pockets of haphazard immigration." Adam's voice was suddenly serious, concerned. "Your country's too close and important to let it get out of control like that. Lots of fresh water and other key resources. The Arctic will become really important by 2050. Russia's already preparing to control its interests in those waters. Canada's a natural land bridge to Alaska. If it hasn't got its act together by the time we're great again, we'll need to do something." He chuckled. "That gal you've got running the Pentagon isn't one to procrastinate long if North America's peace and security are in jeopardy."

Adam wiggled out of his chair and stood tall. The rain had stopped, and tiny ray of late afternoon sun hit the window. "A great job, Carol. Let's call it a day."

He followed Carol out the office door and a happy whistle somehow came through his lips as a cloud of cigar smoke floated toward the ceiling.

THE END

APPENDIX

SOME NON-FICTION BOOKS ON RELATED SUBJECTS

The War That Ended Peace by Margaret MacMillan
Running the World by David Rothkopf
The Revenge of Geography by Robert D. Kaplan
Against All Enemies by Richard A. Clarke
The Great Unraveling by Paul Krugman
Obama and the Middle East by Fawaz A. Gerges
The Money Mafia by Paul T. Hellyer
The Israeli Lobby and U.S. Foreign Policy by John J. Mearsheimer and Stephen M. Walt
The Prize by Daniel Yergin
The Enemy Within by Terry Crowdy
Failed States by Noam Chomsky
The World's Bankers by Sebastian Mallaby
The Balfour Declaration by Jonathan Schneer
The Controversy of Zion by Geoffrey Wheatcroft
Churchill and the Jews by Martin G. Gilbert
Secret Societies by David V. Barrett
The Freemasons by Jasper Ridley
The True Story of the Bilderberg Group by Daniel Estulin
Theft of a Nation by William W. Baker
The Pledge by Leonard Slater
Beyond the Promised Land by Glenn Frankel
By Way of Deception by Victor Ostrovsky
Every Spy a Prince by Dan Raviv and Yossi Melman
Rabin by Leah Rabin
The Volunteer by Michael Boss
Judaism, An illustrated historical overview by Monika Grübel
The Rise and Fall of Jewish Nationalism by Doron Mendels
After Zionism by Naomi Klein
Next Year in Jerusalem by Daphna Golan-Agnon
Witness in Palestine by Anna Baltzer
Israel/Palestine by Tanya Reinhart
Red Notice by Bill Browder
War by Other Means by John J. Fialka
Anti-Judaism: The Western Tradition by David Nirenberg
American Nations by Colin Woodard

Printed in Canada